SUMMER'S ECHO

BOOK FOUR OF THE FOUR PART SERIES SOULLESS

SUMMER SELINE COYLE

S S E Publishing & Acacia Leaf Press. Rothesay

SUMMER'S ECHO

S S E Publishing & Acacia Leaf Press. Rothesay

ISBN 978-1-9994639-4-6

It is not the author's intent to depict a specific region. The particular setting of the novel is not a relevant factor in the narrative. The emphasis is on the universal aspect of the social issues in the book.

This book is a work of fiction. Any similarities to real persons either living or otherwise, and real events are purely coincidental.

Technical support and formatting: Lyla Coyle

SUMMER'S ECHO is the final book in the SOULLESS Series.
Long-denied passions ignite in an all-consuming conflagration,
ending in tragedy. The tender, fragile love between Sydney and
Brett flourishes in the toxic soil of their small town. Sydney's world
eventually comes crashing down around her. Lives collide and
bonds dissolve. An exotic locale holds the key to the past.

LGBTQ THEMES, STRONG LANGUAGE.

"Beautiful descriptions of the different settings in which the novel occurs,
especially the urban and cultural offerings of Istanbul. Straight and gay
relationships are developed with tasteful tact."

The Selective Reader

This book is dedicated to my beautiful daughter Lyla, who is a joy and an inspiration to me.

SUMMER'S ECHO
BOOK FOUR OF THE **SOULLESS** SERIES

Table of Contents

Chapter 1/ LATE SPRING

The words played repeatedly in her head like a slowed-down 45 rpm record. Cymbals and gongs rang out in her ears. Cars swished by in a swirl of headlights, their horns like discordant trombones in a marching band of harbingers of ill will. The rain chilled her to the bone.

Leaning against one of the porch columns to steady herself, she dug around in her shoulder bag for her keys. She let herself into the dark vestibule and pressed the button marked "NO". In the living room, she threw herself on the sofa and buried her head under an oversized toss cushion. The harsh ringing of the telephone demanded her attention. She reached across to the opposite side of the lamp table to pick up the receiver.

"Hi, Mom." the voice on the other end said.

"Toby, what's wrong, hon?"

"Nothing's wrong, Mom. I've got something to tell you: There's somebody here."

"Who, honey?"

"It's Laurie, Mom. She's here with her son."

"Laurie?"

"She's got a little eight month old son, Zenon. She's divorced now."

"Is she moving here?"

"She's just visiting...Actually, she just showed up at the door. I called you before, but you were out."

"I had an appointment. Do you think she'll speak to me?"

"I'll see. Just a sec – okay?"

She could hear him in the background, engaged in a heated discussion.

"Laurie, I've got Mom on the phone. She really wants to talk to you."

"Tell her to keep the fuck away from me."

"Come on. She's our mother."

"She's no fucking mother to me."

"Laurie, you're being really immature. You're holding grudges from way back when we were little kids. That's not fair. Mom's a really good mom. She loves all of us a lot."

"She might be a good mother to the lot of you, but she's never been a good mother to me. She was a fucking drunk and whore."

"Mom always did the best she could for all of us. Why don't you just give her a chance? It's not easy being a mom on your own." this was Keir's voice.

"I can see she's got all of you brainwashed."

"You're so pigheaded. You didn't even want to meet our elder sister, Marin."

"Miss Fucking Goody Two Shoes, the Fucking Golden Child. No thanks."

"Laurie, you have to grow up some time and there's no time like the present." this was Lisa, Keir's fiancée, "She's your mother and she loves you very much. You can't hold on to this 'poor me' attitude forever. Frankly, it's wearing thin. Now that you're a mother yourself, you'll soon realize how difficult it is to raise children."

"Who the fuck do you think you are to judge me, bitch? Who the fuck do all of you think you are? I can see it was a huge mistake to visit my so-called family, to show my son. From now on, you're all fucking dead to me."

"Who cares?" Toby snickered, "Who needs you, anyway?"

"I'm very disappointed in you, Laurie." this was Josh. "I believed becoming a mother yourself would make you more compassionate, but you're as hardened and cold as ever. Maybe it's for the best if you stay away. You'll find out soon enough what the real world is all about."

"Yeah. You'll come crawling back to us." Toby said.

"Don't hold your fucking breath. Fuck you! Fuck you all!"

"Laurie!" Josh called out with authority. "Sit down!"

There was desperate cry of a baby and the slamming of a door.

"Laurie!"

"Let her go, Dad. She's a head case." Keir said.

"Yeah, she's possessed! She needs an exorcist!" Toby said.

"Mom." Keir picked up the phone. "I'm really sorry about that. Laurie's gone off the deep end. I'll call you back soon. Okay?"

"Sure, hon. Love you bunches."

"Love you, Mom."

The words were still echoing in her head:

"I'm so sorry to inform you, Brett...So sorry...I'm so sorry to inform you..."

* * *

Following a mild winter, spring was still struggling to put down roots in early June. Dottie sank her hands deep into the pockets of her long plum cardigan and continued her walk along The Green. When had it all begun to fall apart? When had she lost her footing and fallen into that chasm? She had not seen it coming. Five years of marriage...Five years of memories...all swept away, discarded...Yes, it had ended amicably, people reminded her, not the way other marriages had dissolved, embroiled in custody battles, infidelity, acrimony...It had all been most civilized. They were simply incompatible. There were no children, no financial battles. Despite a lack of prenuptial agreement, (for which, she had been admonished dozens of times by her parents) J.T. had made no financial demands. It had ended as though it had never happened. They had hugged and wept for the very last time. He had loaded his belongings into his friend's pickup truck and driven away to Nova Scotia for a fresh start. Well-meaning mutual acquaintances kept her informed about his activities, emphasizing his lack of romantic partners, just as they most likely informed him of her similar predicament.

She missed the umbrella of her illusions that had sheltered her from the real world as a child. She and Peggy had laughed, played, made crafts and frightened themselves on carnival rides. Now, it was just the four of them left at the mansion: Her, Peggy, Warren and the newly-widowed Maxine, barely keeping the place together, constantly having to hire workers to remedy one old house problem or another, and getting swindled in the process because of the family name. Peggy and Maxine paid a low rent for a suite each and pitched in with the cooking and laundry, while a cleaning service came in once a week. Her father had been forced to dismiss the entire staff. No one on the outside had an inkling about the financial woes visited upon them following Tony's death. He had managed to funnel the majority of the family fortune into Sydney's annuity and yet another surprise annuity: Jack's. His colleagues had been able to arrange provisions for Jack according to his wishes without disclosing his whereabouts to anyone. Tony had planned every minutiae with meticulous care and selected the most trustworthy colleagues to execute his grand plan. He had even made provisions for her.

No one had grieved Mildred's death six months following Tony's. And no one had missed her parents after their permanent move to Victoria, B.C. She had not remained in contact with them, or granted them a passing thought. She felt a sense of calm, at last. She was leading an ordinary life – once, the most unattainable treasure.

Chapter 2/ FORGOTTEN SUMMERS

No more running. No more lies. He was free at last. Free to breathe. Free to be Jack Chandler. If only he could remember whoever Jack Chandler was. He climbed the steep stairs to the dimly lit third floor of the aging, hastily gentrified brick tenement. He opened the door bearing the sign: Dr. Abraham Bloomberg, Psychologist. The stern woman with bifocals and a severe bun at the reception desk acknowledged him with a nod. Behind her, the office door opened and a white-haired man smiled.

"Ah, Jack, come right in."

He closed the door behind them after Jack settled in the black leather chair and glanced around the office at the colorful abstract art on the walls.

"How have things been since our last meeting?" he sat behind his desk facing Jack.

"About the same. Doctor, I was wondering if we should try hypnosis again."

"Considering the traumatic experience you had when we tried it before, I'm hesitant to try it again, Jack. First, you relived being in the fire at your club. Then, you remembered that woman insulting your manhood...What was her name again? Laura?"

"Linda. She's the one who was murdered and I believed for the longest time that I had killed her."

"It was established that she was murdered by her associate; isn't that right?"

"Yes."

"You no longer feel responsible for her predicament, I hope."

"No, I don't."

"Good."

"I still wish I could remember. The only knowledge I have of my life back home is what my friends Aydin and Kent have told me. I still can't remember anything on my own."

"You can't rush these things, Jack. We've still got a long road ahead of us."

"But am I making any progress at all, Doctor? Or is this all in vain? Do you think I waited too long to seek help?"

"It's never too late, Jack. And, yes, you have made progress. You've remembered the night of the fire. You've remembered Linda. You're piecing some facts together."

"I only seem to be remembering the negative things. I want to remember my happy memories. I want to remember my loved ones."

"Have you had any new flashbacks about Sydney?"

"That image of her keeps playing over and over in my head...The one where we're dancing to "I Didn't Know What Time It Was"...I keep seeing her face everywhere."

"Why have you made no attempt to contact her? I understand your hesitation when you were under the mistaken assumption that you were wanted by the police...Also when you were told by the Stephen fellow that you and he were lovers...And when you discovered Sydney had married your cousin...But, now, things are different. Your cousin has passed away. You're no longer down and out. You're financially secure."

"I don't want her to see me like this. I want her to remember me as the man I used to be...The man she loved. She's obviously moved on. She fell in love with my cousin and she was no doubt devastated by his loss. It's too late for the two of us."

"You don't know that. It's been over seven years since you saw her last. Do you still love her?"

"I'll always love Sydney."

"Then, tell her."

"I can't...I want to get better, so I can be deserving of her."

"Then, we have our work cut out for us. How do you feel about the fact that Sydney married your cousin? Do you feel resentful? Betrayed perhaps?"

"No. I'm glad that he was there for her. I'm grateful to him. He's the reason I'm financially stable now. I wish he were still alive, so Sydney could be happy."

"Do you feel undeserving of the money he bequeathed to you?"

"Yes."

"Your cousin apparently cared about you very much. It was his wish that you receive his generous gift."

"He should have lived. He should have had a lifetime with Sydney."

"Jack, you're an extraordinary man. But, my friend, the fact is, your cousin is dead. He wanted you to have this endowment. You need to accept this without guilt. As for Sydney, she has a right to know you're all right and you have some memory of her. I understand you're afraid of being hurt, but..."

"I'm not ready yet. I can't reach out to her like this."

"All right. We can revisit this later...Now, I would like to talk more about the relationships you've had since your tragic circumstances. First, there was Cicely, the nurse. Tell me more about her."

"She was a wonderful girl. I was very happy with her. I really believed we could have had a future. But, as you know, it came to an end when the police showed up at the cabin where she and Ribby were hiding me from Dr. Mazot and my stepmother. I thought the police were after me because I had killed Linda, so I took off."

"Then, you spent some time living on Skid Row...until Stephen found you and convinced you the two of you had been lovers. What was that period like?"

"I was very grateful to Stephen. He rescued me and gave me shelter. He found a job for me."

"How did it feel to be intimate with him? Did you feel any physical attraction?"

"I didn't, but it didn't matter. He was good to me. I owed him. I was committed to him."

"Then, the relationship came to an end."

"Stephen started staying out at nights; then he was staying away for days at a time. We stopped communicating."

"And, that is when your friends informed you about Stephen's deception. How did that make you feel?"

"I was shocked...confused..."

"Were you angry?"

"Hurt, but not angry. I could understand how emotions can get in the way. I'm sure it must've been eating away at him all that time. And, later, when my cousin Tony died and his lawyer was trying to contact me at Stephen's place, thinking we were still a couple, Stephen did the ethical thing and gave him Kent and Aydin's number because they were the only ones who knew where I was. He could've just said he didn't know my whereabouts, but he did the right thing. I have no ill will toward Stephen. I hope he's resting in peace."

"Were you upset when he died?"

"Of course. He was an unwitting victim of this horrific Aids epidemic. He had everything to live for and he was robbed of it."

"After your relationship with Stephen ended, you spent a few years in Idaho and almost got married."

"I thought I could just fly under the radar and live a quiet, unassuming life there, but it didn't work out that way."

"What was your relationship like with the young lady you almost married?"

"It was nice at first. Ellie worked at the local diner. She was a cute, bubbly girl. I went to the diner for my dinner after a long day of working on the farm. She always saved me some apple pie. I really liked her. We dated for a while. I got her pregnant, so I stepped up and asked her to marry me."

"What went wrong?"

"When Stephen was diagnosed with Aids, Kent phoned me and told me I needed to get tested. Ellie needed to get tested, too."

"Both of your results came back negative."

"Yes. But the damage was done. Ellie was fuming, and so were all the other people in the community. They wanted me gone. Some of them tried to run me over with their tractors. Some threatened me with rifles. I had to leave. Ellie had a secret abortion somewhere in another state, so no one would find out she had been carrying a monster's baby."

"Small communities are notoriously racist and homophobic, unfortunately. The idyllic life we seek comes with a high price."

"I came back to New York because, with the money Tony left me, I can afford to live here now. This is the only place where I have friends. The voice and piano lessons I provide for kids in the Bronx give me so much fulfillment."

"If it weren't for Sydney, would you still be trying so hard to remember your past?"

"Probably not. But because of the feelings I experience when I think about her, I desperately want to unlock the memories of her and our relationship."

"Do you feel stuck? Do you feel you can't move on and form a new relationship because of this, as well as because of the negative experiences with Stephen and Ellie?"

"I don't want to be with anyone anymore."

"What if you get your memory back and due to unforeseen circumstances, you can't rekindle what you had with Sydney?"

"If that's the case, I'll have to accept it. She's with me all the time in my heart. She's my guiding star. I want her to be happy. I just want to know who I was, what my life was like, who my friends were. I'm hoping that, as we keep probing, there'll be new memories unearthed."

"Then, that's what we'll do, my friend."

* * *

The taxi sped off in the direction of Lincoln Road to pick up another fare from the airport. She stood in the middle of the driveway, looking toward the main house, its blinds and curtains drawn even on this bright day. Blackened wood peeked out from behind peeling paint. Loose shutters were creaking in the wind. Dying shrubs and overgrown trees concealed the first storey from view. Once a testament to the opulence of Beavertown's privileged class, it now stood humbled by decay. Forlorn and forgotten, the guest house had its wheelchair ramp and black shutters removed. The generously-sized mid-century windows had been replaced with smaller, airtight ones. By the front door, she noticed the modest patch of marguerites, matching the one by the front steps of the main house. She smiled. It was Maxine's signature. She found the key Dottie had placed under the concrete planter of dead geraniums and unlocked the door. She was greeted by the lemony scent of cleaning supplies. Another gesture of kindness from Maxine. She smiled and deposited her lone suitcase and her shoulder bag on the white terrazzo floor. In the living room, she was surprised to find her own furniture, out of storage and freshened up, each piece arranged the way she and Tony had placed it. As she opened the casement windows, she spied two women on the sidewalk pausing to catch a glimpse of her.

"Somebody's livin' there again, Helen. Look. The windows are open."

"That's just Maxine. She's been goin' in there and cleanin' lately."

"There's somebody at the window. She don't look like Maxine to me."

"Doggone it. I think you're right, Hilda. It's that Stanley girl. She must be back. She sure had bad luck with all her husbands, didn't she?"

"What could she be doin' back here, I wonder."

"Lookin' for a new husband!" Helen snickered.

"I wonder who she's gonna marry this time." Hilda joined her laughter.

She moved away from the window, stifling her own laughter. She could still hear them.

"I'm keepin' a close eye on her to see who she picks next. No wonder we can't get any men. She's hoarding them all."

"Can't wait to tell Bea."

She carried her luggage to the bedroom. Everything was the way she and Tony had it before his death and her eviction. She had not expected this considerate gesture. Tears filled her eyes. Dottie and the girls had gone to great lengths to make her feel welcome. She would have to wait until tomorrow to give them their presents and spend uninterrupted time with them. Everyone was at work now. By the time they returned, she would be gone. She would leave a note for them in the mailbox before she left. She opened the bedroom windows and unpacked slowly, savoring each moment of being home again. Birds were singing outside and the scent of lilacs from the neighbor's bush filled the room. She wondered if the phone was activated yet. She had made the arrangements from Toronto and had been informed it would be ready by eleven a.m. the latest. Eli and Daniel had made her promise to call when she arrived safe and sound.

"Hi, Eli. It's me." she said when he answered.

"Hey, pretty lady. We miss you already. Daniel's going to pick up the kitchen extension, so we can both talk to you."

"That would be great."

"Hi, Sydney."

"Hi, Daniel."

"How does it feel to be in Beavertown after five years?"

"I thought it was going to be much harder, but Dottie had a beautiful surprise waiting for me here at the guest house. All the things Tony and I bought together are here, just as we left them. It feels like time stood still."

"That's terrific. I'm not surprised. Dottie adores you." Eli said, "Are you going to see Brett later today?"

"I thought I'd surprise her at the club tonight."

"That's a great idea. She'll be so excited to see you. She really needs your support now with her daughter going missing. I'm glad you decided to be with her at this time."

"I couldn't possibly stay away, Eli."

"You haven't seen her in five years." Daniel said, "Are you nervous?"

"A bit."

"But you've overcome the guilt you had about feeling you had somehow stolen him from her and caused his death."

"That's thanks to five years of therapy with you, Daniel."

"You worked hard during those five years. Give yourself some credit, too, Sydney. You're a strong lady."

"Thank you."

"Enjoy your reunion with her." Eli said, "Keep in touch and take good care of yourself."

"You, too, Eli. You two take care of each other."

"Love you, pretty lady."

"Love you, too."

"We're both here for you any time you want to talk."

"Thank you, Daniel."

She smiled. Eli was in good hands. His accompanying her on her first therapy appointment had led to his fortuitous meeting with his future life partner. She had worried about him moving out of his apartment, however, much to her delight, those fears had been unfounded. Daniel had chosen to move in with Eli and bring only a few treasures of his own. His son and daughter had been bequeathed the majority of all he had collected throughout his life. He had given her two ceramic doves, which she displayed in the small china cabinet in her apartment. It was inspiring to witness a retired editor and a semi-retired psychologist discover love after numerous failed relationships in their younger years.

She undressed, scattering her dress and underwear on the bedroom floor. Maxine had even provided clean towels, shampoo and soap for her in the sparkling clean bathroom. The hot shower was invigorating. She would see Brett at last and they would return to those innocent days before heartaches had visited both of them.

* * *

The club was not as she remembered it. The elegant Art Deco lounge had morphed into a casual, lacklustre modern nightclub. Gone were Johnny O. and Gene And The Matchmakers, replaced by a young, husky D.J. in a booth. A nondescript pop song from the seventies was blaring. Patrons in casual attire were milling around on the dance floor. She recognized no one. Noticing her standing, a young woman with flawless ebony skin in a waitress' uniform approached her with a smile.

"Is there anything I can get you, Ma'am?"

"Yes. I was wondering if Brett Morrow still works here."

"Yes, she does."

"Oh, good." she sighed in relief, "What about Charles Seabrook?"

"He's still here, too. Have you been away from the area for a while?"

She nodded.

"Would you like me to tell Brett you're looking for her, Ms...?"

"No, no. Is she working the early set tonight?"

"Yes. She should be up shortly. Why don't you take a seat? Would you like a drink?"

"Yes. A martini, please."

"Coming right up."

Two older waiters intercepted the young woman on her way back and whispered in her ear, glancing in Sydney's direction. She returned promptly with her drink.

"Here you are, Ms. Goldstein. My name is Cleo, and if there's anything else you'd like, I would be pleased to serve you."

"Thank you, Cleo." she smiled.

The music stopped. Richard emerged jubilantly from the back room, appearing aged and hungover.

"Ladies and Gentlemen, Greene's Lounge presents our own Captain and Tennille: Brett Morrow and Charles Seabrook."

Sydney's heart skipped a beat. She took a large swig of her martini. Chuck took his seat at the piano as a thinner, paler Brett stood beside him. Her wartime-inspired faille dress with a white grid against a black background had cut-away shoulders, a white collar and a silk red rose on her lapel. The snug-fitting bodice emphasized her waiflike figure and flared into a cocktail length circle skirt. Her first number was "Memory" from "Cats".

Sydney felt a light tap on her shoulder and glanced up in surprise. It was Leonard Greene.

"Hello, Sydney. It's lovely to see you." he shook her hand, "After this set, why don't you go down to the dressing room to see Brett?"

"Thank you, Leonard."

"Good to see you."
"You, too. Please give my best to Greeney."

"Will do. Take care." he patted her on the shoulder, "The drinks are on the house."

During Brett's final selection, "MacArthur Park", her eyes met Sydney's. As Brett took her final bow and disappeared behind the curtain, Sydney rose and took the familiar route to the dressing room. Her hands trembling, she knocked softly. Brett opened the door and pulled her into an embrace, shutting the door behind them.

"Brett, I'm so sorry." she buried her face in Brett's fragrant warmth.

"I'm sorry, too, sweetheart." Brett was planting kisses on top of her head.

"Please forgive me, Brett."

"There's nothing to forgive, my Sydney." Brett held her face in her hands, deftly wiping her tears with her fingertips.

Sydney closed a hand over hers and pressed Brett's hand to her lips.

"My little dove." Brett caressed her cheek," You've flown back to me."

"Brett..." she snuggled in close to her, "And, I'm not going anywhere again."

"I have my Sydney back." she molded her own body into hers.

They held each other in silence. Upstairs, the D.J. was playing Peter Cetera's "Hard For Me To Say I'm Sorry".

Chapter 3/ WHAT I DID FOR LOVE

"You don't know how happy it makes me to hear you and Brett are enjoying yourselves, just like old times. Both of you have gone through so much tragedy. You need each other more than ever now."

"I lost so much time being away from her."

"You needed that time to heal and come to terms with your feelings of guilt. Both of you had time to reflect and now you can renew your friendship."

"Thank you for your patience with me during our therapy sessions, Daniel."

"Don't mention it. And you know, I'm always here any time you need to talk. We're like family now."

"Yes. You two are my family."

"Be happy. No one deserves it more than you."

"I appreciate that, Daniel. You and Eli, be happy, too."

"Love you."

"Love you guys."

"Are you seeing Brett tonight?"

"We're going to have a barbeque and watch the Canada Day fireworks from her porch. Chuck is going to be celebrating with us. Then, I'm going to be staying over."

"Enjoy yourself. I'm fixing Eli a special dinner tonight. After that, we'll be staying in. You know what hermits we both are."

"The most lovable hermits in the world. Give my love to my honorary brother."

"He told me to give you his love, too, in case he didn't get back by the time I called you."

"I hope getting his cousin Esther settled in her seniors' apartment went well. I'm so glad Eli has you in his life."

"Thank you. Take care of yourself, pretty lady."

"You, too, Daniel."

So much healing had taken place, so many questions answered, so many fears and doubts put to rest during their time apart. Now she could face Brett. She could remember her therapy sessions with Daniel in such precise detail, it was like turning on a tape recorder to revisit them in order to give herself permission to be happy again.

* * *

"Tell me about Brett."

"Brett...She's an incredible person...One in a million...There's no one like her."

"You care very deeply about her, don't you?"

"I'd give up my life for her."

"And, you feel guilty for falling in love with Tony, her long-time love interest."

"I was selfish and needy. I clung on to Tony like a life preserver."

"You were in pain."

"That doesn't make it all right."

"Had the two of them not already ended their relationship as a result of Lea's pregnancy?"

"Yes, but, deep down, I'm sure they still had feelings for each other."

"If Brett had told you she still loved him and wanted you to break things off with him, would you have done so?"

"In a heartbeat. But she would never do something like that."

"From what you've told me earlier, it appears she practically handed him to you on a silver platter. She gave you her blessing."

"That's the kind of person Brett is. Self-sacrificing."

"I'm sure Tony had a say in it. No one forced his hand. After all, he made the first move, did he not?"

"He was feeling lonely and vulnerable, as well."

"You were there for each other. You made each other happy."

"If I had released him, he would've been back together with Brett as before. She was the love of his life. Not me. They had an open relationship for many years, but always found their way back to one another. I was never meant to be anything more than just another fling for him."

"Obviously, he didn't see it that way. He thought you were special. And, Brett wanted him to be with you. Sydney, you need to accept that. You are not to blame for anything. I don't know how I can get you to see that. You can't carry the weight of other people's pain on your shoulders."

* * *

"Tell me more about your relationship with Tony. How did it evolve? Had you been experiencing feelings for him for some time, but denied them because of your loyalty to Brett?"

"I wasn't aware of any feelings...I thought of him as a friend. I had known him for years as Brett's love interest. Romantic feelings had never entered my mind."

"What changed?"

"When Brett told him to dance with me at Dottie's graduation, I realized my attraction, being so close to him for the first time, but I blocked it out. Then, everything changed the day Brett sent him looking for me at The Admiral."

"We're going to revisit the earlier part of that day when you're ready. For now, let's focus on the subject at hand. How did things change that night?"

"He was attentive, caring...It was genuine...Not just a favor to Brett. That was unexpected."

"How so?"

"I thought he'd be annoyed...Anxious to do his duty and get home...But, instead, he said that he wanted to be with me...That he didn't want me to be alone."

"And it felt right for you."

"Yes, it felt so right. Both of us were lonely...lost...in pain...But when we found each other, we were on top of the world. I know how it might seem to other people...That we were on the rebound, or acting out of neediness and lust, that it couldn't possibly be love...But I really did love him. I wanted a lifetime with him. I should've known his family would do something sinister to destroy our happiness. I underestimated him. Had he not become involved with me and married me, he'd still be alive today."

"He made the decision to defy his family and build a life with you. He loved you and he was happy with you. Without you in his life, he would've remained a slave to *family tradition and a life he did not want. I believe he was happier with you than he had ever been in his life. He would never want you to feel guilty in any way."*

"How can I not feel guilty? I cause harm to everyone I love. First, Jack...Then, Tony..."

"How did you cause harm to Jack?"

"He left Linda because of me and she burnt down his club – a lifelong dream he had built up from scratch...Then, his mother took him to that mad psychiatrist Mazont or Mazolt or whatever his name was, to mess with his mind and cause him brain damage, just to keep him away from me. I cause heartbreak and suffering everywhere I go. My parents had to leave town because my mom's sister and my dad's best friend turned against them when I took Warren to court. I even destroyed Warren's career."

"Sydney, you are not to blame for other people's actions and their consequences. All you did was fall in love with two men from a very dysfunctional family. You need to accept that."

"I must sound like a broken record."

"That's all right. We're going to keep circling around this and repeating the same narrative as many times as we need to, until you stop feeling guilty. There is a school of thought that believes everyone's exit is predetermined. If Tony's time on this realm was predetermined to end on that day, then, he would have died, no matter what. Had he not met you and fallen in love with you, perhaps, he would have died in an accident, or ended his own life for other reasons, one being choosing a woman his family approved of and as a result, feeling so unhappy and trapped that his life lost all meaning...You are not to blame for anything. Remember that, Sydney."

* * *

"Let's talk about Jack. In light of what you learned from your cousin Dottie, did your feelings change?"

"Drastically. All that time, I had been under the impression that he had regained his memory and chosen Stephen over me. I was carrying around feelings of rejection and hurt. Then, I found out he had not been suffering from a temporary fugue state, but permanent brain damage with no chance of ever regaining his memory. I have to accept the fact that what we shared is lost to him and he is lost to me."

"Even so, did you consider searching for him and trying to establish some sort of new relationship with him?"

"I didn't want to cause him pain and confusion. I wanted him to move on and build a fulfilling life for himself. He did not need an albatross around his neck, so I had to release him."

"Do you still love him?"

"I'll always love Jack. Always."

* * *

"You chicks want a hand with those dishes?" Chuck called out from the hallway.

"You did all the grilling. Now it's our turn to work." Brett said, "There isn't much, anyway. Just sit down and relax, hon."

"I see you've still got Friday's newspaper. Maybe I'll get a chance to finally read it." he said.

"We'll be done by the time you read the comics." Brett said, handing the salad bowl to Sydney to be dried.

"This was such a nice day." Sydney said.

"Having you here made it so much nicer for me." she caressed her cheek with a soapy hand and touched the tip of her nose, leaving behind a small bubble.

Sydney dipped her index finger into the sudsy water in the sink and deposited a corresponding bubble on Brett's nose. Both giggled.

"You're wearing your locket and your Star Of David again!" Brett exclaimed, "I never noticed it before. You haven't been able to wear them since the fire. I'm glad you were able to get them repaired."

"They were so badly damaged in the fire that I couldn't find a jeweller all these years who could repair them. During one of my therapy sessions with Daniel, I mentioned them and he said he knew someone who could make them like new. They're never coming off again."

"That's wonderful, hon. And thank you again for this beautiful necklace." she caressed the gold letters of her name in a cursive font with a diamond embedded inside the "B".

"It looks so beautiful on you."

Brett kissed her cheek.

"We're all done here now." Sydney removed the sink stopper, wrung out the dish rag and placed it over the faucet. She folded the dish towel and hung it from the three prong towel rack beside the small window.

"I poured you chicks some coffee." Chuck said as they joined him in the living room.

"Thanks, hon." Brett sat beside him and motioned to Sydney to sit on her other side.

"That's quite stylish." he eyed her necklace, "You're so old, you can't remember your own name. You have to wear it around your neck to remind yourself."

"My Sydney had it custom made just for me by the finest jeweller in Toronto."

"That's because she knows your brain's going."

She was laughing so hard, tears were streaming down her face.

"She also gave me a beaded evening bag and this beautiful blouse for my birthday." once she composed herself, Brett looked down at her black chiffon off-the-shoulder blouse.

"I was there – remember? It was your hundred and fourth birthday."

Her cheeks crimson from laughter, Brett buried her face in Sydney's chest.

"You can wear see-through tops because there's nothing to see through them." Chuck said, still poker-faced, "Thanks again, Syd, for the cigars and the tie clip."

"I looked for a cowboy hat like the one you liked, but had no luck."

"That was kind of you." he smiled paternally, "You didn't have to go to so much trouble."

"No trouble."

"I think I hear a rumble. The fireworks are starting." Brett said, wiping her tears of laughter with a tissue, "I had no idea how late it was."

"No wonder. You fed us all that scrumptious food after the barbeque and the garden salad. We spent hours devouring your saffron rice, cheese pastries, crab salad, and your delicious chocolate cake." Chuck said.

The three of them stepped out to the front porch and leaned over the railing for an unobstructed view of the fairgrounds. Moths flocked to the jam jar porch light and landed on the brown clapboard siding, spreading rice-paper wings.

"I don't like this new shade of brown your landlord painted the house." Chuck remarked, "It looks like baked beans. Every time I look at it, I feel like having a fart."

Their laughter rang out in the still night air. Even the park was silent under the canopy of stars.

"What's taking them so long?" Chuck said, "They had a false start and dragged us outside; now they're keeping us waiting. Brett, why don't you have those little paper flags all over your porch? Where's your patriotism?"

With a loud boom, a cascade of white light rendered them awe-struck. The sky ablaze with red and white shooting stars, Sydney stood beside Brett, feeling Brett's arm encircling her shoulder. Bathed in the bliss of the moment, she thought her heart would leap out of her chest.

Chapter 4/ THROUGH THE FIRE

The ominous sound of the telephone caught her off-guard; the bag of groceries she was carrying into the kitchen slipped out of her hand and fell to the floor with a thud.

"Shit." she picked up the receiver, attempting to untangle the ridiculously shortened cord attached to the mint green wall phone, "Hello?"

"Hey, Syd, do you know where Brett is?" Richard demanded.

"No. I thought she'd be at the club. She was going to visit Maggie at the nursing home this afternoon. She was planning to get changed when she got back and go straight to the club."

"That dumb broad's a no-show."

"That's not like her."

"I don't know why the boss keeps that useless bimbo on. Can you do the early set in her place?"

"Normally, I would, but I think I should go and see if she's all right. I'm sure there's a very good reason for her absence. Can you get Dustin?"

"I suppose so. We prefer to get him for the later sets. All the old fogies who come out to hear yous broads leave early, so we bring out the kid to sing more contemporary stuff for the younger audience."

"Can you make an exception for tonight? He's a good-looking guy; I'm sure the older ladies would enjoy listening to him. Maybe Darrell can D.J. during the late set."

"Looks like I've got no choice. She'd better have a real good excuse. If she leaves me in the lurch like this again, I'm gonna fire her lazy ass."

"Richard, Brett's always been very dependable. I'm sure there's a legitimate reason for her absence. I'm going to check on her to see if she's okay."

"Fine. Tell her she'd better not pull another stunt like this again, or she's fired."

"Good-bye, Richard." she hung up the phone, only to hear it ringing again.

"Richard, what is it now?" she snapped.

"Sydney, it's me, Toby." the frantic voice on the other end informed her, "I've been trying to get a hold of you for ages."

"I'm sorry, Toby. I was out running errands and getting my groceries. Then, the moment I got in, Richard called me, demanding to know where your mom is. Toby, is she all right?"

"I don't think she is. That's why I called you. Dad got a call at work this morning: Laurie and Zenon were killed in an accident in California."

"Toby! I'm so sorry!"

"Apparently, Laurie's car was hit head on by a train. She and the baby were killed instantly. Their bodies were mangled beyond recognition. We called Mom repeatedly but she was out. Dad eventually got a hold of her and went over there to tell her. She's taking it hard. She sent him away and said she wanted to be alone. She's not answering her phone. We're worried she might do something to harm herself."

"I was just on my way over there now."

"I can drive you. It would be a lot quicker."

"Thanks, Toby. I'll wait for you outside."

Toby sped through every red light during the drive to Brett's house. Sydney rang the doorbell repeatedly, knocked, and called out Brett's name while Toby shouted: "Mom, can you hear us?"

"I have no choice but to use my own key." Sydney said.

"I think you should." Toby agreed.

They entered the dark, musty foyer. Only the fronds of the Boston fern were visible in the sliver of light from the streetlamp.

"Brett!" Sydney called out, turning on the lights one by one and looking into each room, "Brett, honey, are you all right?"

She pressed the two-way switch at the bottom of the stairs, and called out to her again. Faint footsteps were heard overhead.

"Mom!" Toby attempted to run up the stairs.

"She may not be decent." Sydney touched his shoulder to detain him.

"Toby, sweetheart," Brett's voice was heard, "Please go back home. I'll be fine. Sydney's here."

"Okay."

"I love you very much, hon."

"I love you, too, Mom. Are you sure you're okay?"

"I will be. You don't have to worry. Sydney's with me. She'll take good care of me."

“Okay.”

“Drive carefully, sweetheart.”

“Yes, Mom.”

“Thanks for giving me a drive, Toby. Your mom’s going to be all right. I’ll take care of her.” Sydney reassured him.

“Bye, guys.” he walked out, locking the door behind him.

Sydney started up the stairs. Brett was leaning against the wall, clad in a cream satin and lace negligee, her mascara running down her cheeks. The stench of alcohol was overpowering on the stuffy upper floor.

“Oh, Brett.” Sydney embraced her, “I’m so sorry, sweetheart. I just found out from Toby.”

“Thank you for being here.”

“I’m always going to be here for you, Brett.”

“I drank two quarts of vodka. I thought I might be able to drink myself into oblivion, but I couldn’t even manage to do that.”

With an arm around her, Sydney led her to the bedroom and tucked her into bed.

“I’ll get you some black tea and soda crackers. Your stomach may not be so kind in the morning.”

“I just want to go to sleep and never wake up.”

“Oh, sweetheart...” Sydney caressed her hair and kissed her forehead, “Why don’t you try to have something? I’ll go down and see what you’ve got in the kitchen.”

“Okay, hon.”

Downstairs, Sydney put on the tea kettle and placed a tea bag in a white mug. She found green seedless grapes in the refrigerator, washed them, and placed them in a white bowl. She carried a wooden tray containing the grapes and a box of crackers up to Brett, and returned for the tea. She propped her up in bed with pillows and sat beside her.

"I'm going to feed these grapes to you one by one." Sydney placed the first one in Brett's mouth.

"I don't know what I'd ever do without you."

"You never have to find out."

"I'd like to plant a tree for Laurie and the baby." Brett spoke up suddenly, "I need to do something for her. I couldn't be with her when she needed me most. It's probably best to plant it in front of Josh's house. She was happy there once – before the divorce. Laurie wasn't always like this. She was a good girl once."

"I think it's a lovely thought. We'll plant it together. What type of tree did you have in mind?"

"Something sturdy. Not a decorative, flimsy thing that will wither and die. I want something that will live long after we're all gone." Brett circled the warm mug with her hands, "Some day, I hope one of the boys will be living in that house and raising a family. They'll tell their kids about Laurie...An oak...What do you think about an oak, Sydney?"

"An oak is strong. It provides shade. Produces acorns for the squirrels. It would be my choice, too."

"We'll plant it in late summer or early fall."

Sydney removed the tray from the bed and placed it on the small steamer trunk across the room.

"I must reek of alcohol." Brett sighed.

"No, you don't." she leaned down to kiss her cheek, "Would you like me to give you a sponge bath to cool you down?"

"That would be lovely, hon."

In the bathroom, Sydney found a metal wash basin, which she filled with warm water and placed on a side table in the bedroom. She later returned to the room with a pink facecloth and a bar of pink Camay soap. A pink towel was slung over her shoulder. She deftly removed Brett's stale negligee. She competently began stroking the facecloth over Brett's face, throat, neck, arms and back, drying her off at intervals. Then, she refreshed the facecloth and sponged her stomach, yet hesitated to touch her breasts. Brett enclosed her hand in her own and led her gently. When it was time to wash the inevitable tuft of downy hair, Sydney's hands were trembling. Brett guided her gently, aware that she was looking away. Sydney took the supplies back to the bathroom. When she returned, she was still unable to meet Brett's eyes.

"I'll get you some fresh clothes." she murmured without turning around.

"Don't bother, hon. It's too hot." Brett crossed the room to her, "Sydney, honey, what's wrong? You went all quiet all of a sudden." Brett's arms enveloped her from behind.

"Don't mind me." Sydney turned around, her eyes tightly shut, "We're going to get through this together, Brett. I'll be by your side every step of the way."

"Sydney...Look at me, sweetheart." Brett brushed away wayward tendrils from Sydney's face, "You're trembling."

Sydney's eyes remained closed. Brett kissed away the tears streaming down her cheeks and pulled her into an embrace. Sydney melted into her arms. Brett's mouth sought hers with raw hunger. Sydney moaned and kissed her with such fervor that Brett was rendered breathless.

"Sydney, I need you so much…" Brett kissed her again and pulled off her black tank top over her head; she unhooked her black lace bra and tugged at the elasticized waist of her black circle skirt, sliding it down past her hips.

"Brett…" Sydney moaned; she tossed her bra, let her skirt fall to the floor, lowered her panties and stepped out of them.

Brett took her hand and led her back to the bed. She slid on top of her and planted tender kisses on her face, her neck and breasts. Her skillful fingers moved lower, navigating every gentle curvature, every mound, every crevice of Sydney's body. Her touch was self-assured, and her passion unbridled. Her mouth explored her salty challis. Sydney's screams of ecstasy filled the humid air and her tears came in a torrent.

Sydney's touch was tentative, shy, tender. She unleashed her long-denied longing. They disintegrated into a quivering mass. The glow from the streetlamp, creeping in through the crack in the drapes illuminated Brett's skin.

"I hope I didn't disappoint you, Brett."

"Disappoint me? You were absolutely exquisite, my angel. I couldn't get enough of you."

"I love you so much, Brett."

"My beautiful Sydney…What did I ever do to deserve you?"

"I'm the one who should be saying that."

"Don't ever say that." she took both of Sydney's hands and pressed them to her lips, "I love you. Do you know how long I've waited for this? How I thought it would never happen? I remember all those nights watching you sleep beside me...I wanted you so much, I thought I'd lose my mind."

"When I watched you with others, I wanted to die. I knew I could never measure up."

"None of them meant anything to me. You were all I wanted. I lay awake nights longing for you. No one's ever meant as much to me as you, Sydney."

"You're everything to me, Brett."

"Where do we go from here, my love?" Brett caressed her hair, "We've stepped over that line to the point of no return. I don't think I can ever let you go now."

"Don't let me go. I don't want you to let me go. I don't want this to end. I never imagined you could want me, too."

"We're in for a rough ride, my angel. We have to lie to everyone around us – even those who are near and dear to us. We're going to be facing soul-crushing oppression from every direction. We'll need to look over our shoulders constantly."

"I'm prepared to face anything, just to be with you, Brett. I can handle anything they throw at me. I'd gladly give up everything for a life with you. Do you think I'm going to let the small-minded homophobes in this toxic little town tear us apart?"

"No one can tear us apart." Brett said, "I wish time could stand still...I wish it could be this summer forever and we could be frozen in time like this."

They reached out to one another over and over through the night. In this unexpected explosion of her senses, Sydney's tentative touch gave way to raw passion. Every inch of Brett's body was as familiar to her as her own now. When they finally collapsed in sheer exhaustion, it was sunlight creeping in through the crack in the drapes. Limbs intertwined, bodies moist, they clung to one another.

"How many times do you think we did it?"

"I lost count hours ago." Brett laughed softly, "We had to make up for lost time."

"I want to shut the world out and hold you like this forever."

"That's what I want, too." Brett nuzzled into her and closed her eyes, "I feel I've finally come home. I can stop running. I've found everything I've ever wanted."

Brett drifted off to sleep. Reveling in her good fortune, Sydney watched her chest heaving with each breath. Brett was hers at long last. She could still taste Brett's skin, smell her ocean, and hear her moans and cries. Even in her wildest dreams, she had never imagined it possible to look into those smoldering dark eyes and see them shimmering with such love. In the lavender-scented dampness of Brett's boudoir, she wept tears of joy.

Chapter 5/ I WANT TO LIVE

"Doctor, I've changed my mind about having the cancer treatment."

"But...The last time..."

"I know what I said at the time. But things have changed since then. I want to live."

"Brett...The thing is...Even if you were to start treatment now, it would make very little difference. It might give you a few extra months. Best case scenario, it might give you another three months. But, your quality of life would be reduced drastically. Of course, the final decision is yours. I'm sorry I cannot give you more hope...But cervical cancer is one of the most pervasive cancers."

"Did I...wait too long? Would it have made a difference if I had started treatment when you first told me?"

"You might have had maybe another six months, but that's all...It's too advanced at this stage. I'm very sorry, Brett...I wish I could offer you more hope."

Her head was spinning. His young, earnest face, the antiseptic smell of the office with the pale green walls, the stark white of his crisp smock were making her nauseated. She stumbled on her way out to the reception area and walked away without a word. Her feet, as though detached from her body, led her down Rookwood Avenue to Wilmot Park. The crushing weight of the rock in her chest threatened to stifle her last breath. Past the bandstand, the house was visible through the network of maples and elms. She paused to catch her breath. The front door opened and Sydney stepped out to the porch. Leaning on the railing, she was craning her neck to catch a glimpse of Brett returning from her appointment. Revitalized by this vision, Brett resumed her weary journey past the trees into the clearing. When Sydney caught a glimpse of her, her face lit up. She ran down the front steps with the exuberance of a child who had spied the ice cream man. Arms open, she ran across the park to embrace her.

"Are you all right, sweetheart?"

"I am, now, baby."

"I wish you had let me go with you."

"This was something I needed to take care of alone."

Sydney did not question her. With an arm through hers, she led her back to the house.

"I'm afraid things did not go the way I'd hoped." Brett threw herself on the sofa.

Sydney brought in two steaming mugs of tea. She placed an ottoman in front of Brett and helped her put her feet up. As she was about to return to the kitchen for muffins, Brett reached out to touch her arm.

"Please stay here, sweetheart. I need to talk to you."

With growing trepidation, Sydney sat beside her.

"I don't know how to tell you this...I should've told you before, but I was hoping against hope that I could change the outcome..."

"Brett, what is it? You're scaring me."

"I'm scared, too, sweetheart."

"No matter what it is, we can face it together."

"Oh, Sydney, I can't find the words to tell you."

"It's okay...It's okay..." Sydney held her and kissed away her tears.

In the shelter of her arms, Brett wept inconsolably.

"Sydney, I'm dying." she blurted out suddenly.

Sydney froze. Brett pulled away from her to hold her face in her hands.

"No...No...Tell me it's not true...Brett, tell me it's not true...They've made a mistake...They've got your lab results mixed up with someone else's...It happens all the time...They're going to call you and tell you it was a mistake."

"I'm afraid not, sweetheart." Brett pulled her to herself, "I thought I could extend my time if I agreed to the treatments, so I could have better news for you...But, the doctor said it would only make a negligible difference."

"How long did he say we have?"

"A year."

"And with the treatment?"

"Another three months at the most, but with decreased quality of life from the side effects."

"We can look into alternative therapies...Macrobiotic diet, holistic healing...We can make the most of the time we have together. How long have you known?"

"Since the day Laurie went missing...I had just returned from the doctor's office when Toby called me to tell me Laurie was there with the baby. The boys tried to get her to talk to me, but she refused and took off. I hope she's at peace now. Maybe she can find a way to forgive me."

"You haven't done anything you need to be forgiven for, Brett."

"I've done plenty. Now I'm paying the price."

"Don't talk like that."

"Cervical cancer is caused by HPV, a sexually transmitted virus. My lifestyle caused this."

"HPV doesn't care how many partners you've had. You could catch it even if you've only had one partner."

"I don't know what I ever did to deserve you, hon." Brett held her hand, "I've got my affairs in order. I went to see Marcel, Tony's trusted colleague and friend, right away. I've been squirrelling away some money, a little bit here and there, for Marin and Brettiella. Keir and Toby are to get some family heirlooms and the rest of my personal effects are to go to Marin. Do you think that's fair?"

"Very fair. The boys are going to be receiving an inheritance from Josh, but Marin doesn't have a dad."

"I want you to have my records, tapes, sheet music and piano, and any clothes, jewellery, accessories, knickknacks, books, and furniture you fancy. If you don't tell me which ones, I'll pick them out for you."

"Please don't feel you need to give me anything."

"You don't get to say 'no'. Either you pick out what you want, or you get stuck with what I pick out for you."

"Brett, please..."

"This was always my plan."

"I don't want to think about any of this. I can't live without you, Brett. Please take me with you. Please."

"Oh, my darling..." Brett enclosed her in her intoxicating warmth, "My Sydney...I am so filled with you...I had never imagined this much love between two people."

"I can't let you go. I don't want to live if you're not with me."

"Life needs to go on for you, Sydney. You must promise me you'll move on after I'm gone. I need to know you're going to be all right."

"No! Brett, don't say that!"

"I want you to move on with someone else and find happiness. That's my wish for you."

"I can't do that."

"We'll make the most of the time we have left. We'll live each moment to the fullest. Summer is a short season, my beautiful Sydney. We must hold on to summer. This summer belongs to us."

As Sydney held her close, the pain of Brett's loss was already settled within her. Upstairs, as she made love to her with unbridled passion, she allowed herself to pretend summer would never be stolen from them.

Chapter 6/ GOD ONLY KNOWS

Two oversized trash bags filled with empty liquor bottles were propped up against the back door. Sydney had emptied their contents into the sink the previous night.

"Alcohol is a carcinogen. Cancer cells feed off the sugar in it. Coffee and sweets are also off-limits from now on. I'm going to follow the same diet restrictions as you." she had told her.

"I'm off now, sweetheart." Sydney slung her handbag across her shoulder, and called up the stairs, "I'll take the bags to the bottle exchange on my way to the supermarket."

The persistent ringing of the doorbell took them by surprise.

"Who could that be so early in the day?" Brett called out from the bathroom as she flushed the toilet.

"I'll take care of it." Sydney attempted to catch a glimpse through the glass in the door, however, the visitor was standing to one side and concealed from view; she opened it reluctantly.

A disheveled Josh brushed past her brusquely.

"Where's Brett?"

Not waiting for a response, he barged into the living room as Brett was descending the stairs.

"I just got into town this morning. The boys told me. Are you all right, babe?" he grabbed Brett's elbows.

"I'm just fine."

"We'd like some privacy." Josh glared at Sydney.

"Josh, don't speak to Sydney that way!"

"It's okay, Brett. I have to run those errands, anyway."

"You don't have to come back." Josh said, "I'm here now. I'll take care of her."

"I don't want you to do that, Josh. I want Sydney with me."

"You need medical attention. You need someone strong and capable in charge."

"That someone is Sydney. It's my health and my decision."

"She's unhealthy for you. She smothers and devours you. It's an unnatural, unsavory relationship. You're vulnerable and she's taking advantage of that."

"Josh, I want you to leave!" Brett ordered, pointing to the front door, "And, don't come back here with your venom."

"Brett..."

"I mean it: Go away."

"I'm not going anywhere. She needs to pack up and move out."

"You heard her. She doesn't want you." Sydney glared at him, "Now, sling your hook."

"Someone needs to protect her from a vulture like you." Josh shot back at her.

"You're the vulture." Brett pushed him away, "I want you to leave now, Josh."

"You need me, babe."

"I haven't needed you for a long time, Josh."

"I'm not going to back down without a fight. If you don't get rid of her, I will. And I can't promise I'll be gentle. No woman can give you what I can."

"No man can give me what Sydney can. You stay away from her, or you'll answer to me!"

"It's just another passing infatuation. You lust after anything that moves. Your bed is so hot, I'm surprised it hasn't caught fire. Half the population of Beavertown's been there. If you weren't dying, you'd toss her aside, too, like the others, once you grew tired of her."

"Get out! Get out!" Brett shoved him toward the door, summoning all of her strength and slammed it behind him after forcing him out.

"He's a piece of work." Sydney said.

"A real douchebag. I'm sorry you had to put up with that, sweetheart."

"I think he got the message. I'd better get going." she looked away to conceal her moistened eyes.

"Sweetheart, please don't go yet."

"It's okay, Brett."

"No, it's not. I will not allow anyone to treat you that way." she kissed her, "Sydney, I love you in a way I've never experienced with anyone before. I want it to be just us. I want to shut everything and everyone out. In this imperfect world, we have to hang on to what we hold dear."

Overcome by tears, Sydney disintegrated into Brett's protective arms.

"I've been searching for you all my life." Brett caressed her back, "The moment I laid eyes on you, I knew you were the one. But I realized I had to tread gently. I didn't want to lose you."

"You couldn't have lost me, Brett. I wanted you, too."

"All those years, I was so afraid of scaring you away if I revealed I was head over heels in love with you."

"I was head over heels for you, too, Brett, and terrified of losing you if you ever found out."

"The love that dared not speak its name." Brett murmured wistfully.

"Now we're together and no one can come between us." Sydney kissed her hands and led her to the sofa.

"Except the Grim Reaper."

"I've struck up a deal with him: If he's going to take you, he has to take me, too. We're a pair. He can't break up a set."

"Sweetheart..."

"It's a done deal. You don't have a say in it."

"Then, I'm going to smother you with so much love, you'll be itching to get away from me."

"I would love to be smothered by you. You won't get any complaints from me. And, watch out, I'm going to be smothering you, too."

"That's perfect. I'd love to be smothered by you, too."

"When love is this intense, it's inevitable that both people smother each other with affection. I don't understand those who complain about not having breathing room. When you have this much love, everything is enhanced and lived on a higher level."

"I've dreamt of experiencing this all-encompassing love with you. It's so rare, and so few ever find it. We're among the most fortunate."

"Society says we have to hang our heads in shame. But I'll always hold my head up high." she nestled into Brett's arms and they remained that way in a comforting silence.

Opening her eyes as the clock struck noon, Sydney rose and retrieved the clinking trash bags from the kitchen.

"I'm going to get those errands out of the way, so I can prepare a special meal for you."

"I can't wait." Brett walked her to the door.

"Love you." Sydney blew her a kiss.

"Love you, too." Brett blew her a kiss of her own and watched her until she turned the corner.

*　*　*

Brett concluded her set with the Beach Boys' song "God Only Knows", took a bow and joined Sydney backstage in the cramped room behind the curtain. Chuck's voice could be heard from the hallway.

"I'll be back after I take the chicks home."

"Make sure you're back in time for Dustin's set." Richard demanded, "Why can't they take a cab like they used to?"

"They're just getting their coats, not changing their clothes, so it'll be quick."

"I don't know why the boss put them on split sets every night instead of full sets on alternating nights. The patrons don't like it. They come on certain nights to hear either one or the other. When you get a chance, you should talk to the boss about that."

"It's his decision. I'm sure he has his reasons. He's the boss. He can do whatever he wants." he retorted, "You chicks come out to the car when you're ready." he called out in a louder voice.

Muttering unintelligibly under his breath, Richard walked away, the diminuendo of his heavy footsteps trailing off down the hall. Darrell put on Stevie Wonder's song "Overjoyed". With a hand on her arm to steady her, Sydney led Brett down the stairs to the dressing room.

"Are you all right?" she asked her.

"A little more tired than usual, hon. I need to catch my breath for a second." she sat down with her back to the vanity mirror.

Sydney knelt in front of her. Her fingers danced up Brett's legs, to her thighs, and higher, caressed her over her pantyhose. Brett moaned softly. Neither one heard the opening of the door. Richard's gruff voice crudely brought their pleasure to an end.

"I should've known! I should've known a couple of kooks like yous two would be dykes! That does it! Yous dames are fired! I don't want yous giving the place a bad rep. People are going to think this is one of them clubs for queers!" his face beet red, he shook an index finger in their direction, "Clear out all your stuff and don't ever darken this door again! Anything yous leave behind will be tossed in the trash. Your final cheques will be in the mail. Make sure you turn in your keys." he slammed the door behind him.

"I'm so sorry, Brett. This is all my fault."

"No, sweetheart; it was just a matter of time before he figured it out, anyway. At least, now, we don't have to put on an act in front of people. It takes way too much energy to pretend."

"It would've been later instead of sooner if I had been able to control my urges."

"He had no business barging in like that."

"Chuck told him we weren't changing our clothes, so he figured we'd be decent."

"He sure got an eyeful." Brett laughed, "I'll bet he wanted to join."

"I'm sure he did." Sydney laughed shyly.

"Well, baby, we're out of work, out of luck, and out of time."

"Don't worry. I can cover the rent, the bills, and all that. This gives us more time together and you can conserve your energy for more important things."

"I don't want you to be in that position, Sydney."

"I want to do it. Come on, let's get our coats and get out of here. I can come back for our stuff tomorrow." she put on her coat and helped Brett with hers, "I'm planning to sell the contents of the guest house, anyway, to an auction house. It won't bring in much, but I'd rather make less with a reputable buyer than risk dealing with shady unknown people out there. It's all stuff Tony and I bought together when we got married. I'll see which pieces Dottie and the girls like, so I can gift them before I sell the bulk of the stuff. But, first, why don't we go there and see if there are some pieces you'd like to bring back with us?" she locked the door behind them, as they walked toward the stairs.

"That sounds lovely, hon." Brett kissed her.

Upstairs, they walked proudly past Richard, the servers and the customers with linked hands and stepped outside to Chuck's waiting car.

Chapter 7/ YOU GO TO MY HEAD

The cleansing water washed away Brett's tears and trickled down her right shoulder and arm as she pressed herself against the cold white tile. With one hand on Brett's left arm and the other on her right hip, Sydney was planting tender kisses on her neck, shoulders, and breasts, sucking on her tiny, pale peach nipples. She slid her right hand from Brett's arm, and reached lower. Brett grasped her shoulders. Sydney's fingers followed that ever so familiar path, sending Brett into cries of rapture. Pressing closer into her, she moved rhythmically with Brett's tremors. Struck aware of how fragile, how weightless her body felt in her arms, she held onto her.

Brett's mouth sought hers with raw hunger. Sydney moaned. Writhing with pleasure as Brett caressed her, she held onto her urgently.

"Sydney, open your eyes." Brett murmured, "I want to look in your eyes when you come."

Brett's skillful fingers navigated toward their final destination, sending jolts of electricity through her. They held onto each other in a prolonged tearful embrace. Sydney turned off the shower and stepped out of the tub first; she helped Brett step onto the furry pink mat. They dried each other off with mint green towels and tossed them on the floor.

They ran, naked, down the hall, with the giddy exhilaration of schoolgirls, dripping water on the hardwood floors, and collapsed on the bed, laughing.

"Your landlord's not going to be too happy about the damage that water's going to do to the wood floor."

"Too bad for him. The old goat keeps raising my rent. He can well afford to have the floor refinished. He's going to be plenty pissed about the condition of this whole place, anyway. My Toby's put more wear and tear into this house over the years than all the people who lived here in the past century."

"Isn't he some rich businessman with a fancy house in Skyline Acres?"

"Yeah. Mr. Charm School. Struts his stuff like Marlon Brando."

"Does he look like him?"

"He wishes."

Sydney burst into laughter.

"Speaking of Charm School dropouts, I'm relieved Richard's out of the club." Brett said, "Leonard really pulled through for us, reinstating us and firing Richard. I think Cleo will do an amazing job as the new manager."

"I think so, too."

"I'm just worried about what he might do to retaliate."

"You leave him to me, Brett."

"I'm worried about the damage people like Richard and Josh can do to you, sweetheart. I'm going to be dead and gone, but you have to live here. I don't want you to become a social pariah."

"I already am. No matter what I do, people resent me."

"Sweetheart, you can't take on the world. I can't bear to see what our love is doing to you. Homophobic rednecks are everywhere."

"It's you and me against the world. They can't hurt us with their ignorance and hate. Our love is strong enough to defeat them."

"Oh, my darling." a somber expression swept across her face, "My dearest love."

Lying in Brett's scented bosom, intoxicated by her lovemaking, at that moment, she felt invincible.

* * *

"You know, dear, I'm afraid there's going to be a time when I won't be able to work at all." Brett was telling Leonard backstage.

"We'll cross that bridge when we get to it." Leonard reassured her, "We're auditioning for a female singer now. She'll fill in when you don't feel up to coming in. We'll eventually transition her into the early set. Don't push yourself too hard, Brett. If you need to take some time off, let me know. I can arrange the schedule around you. And the same goes for you, Sydney. You're a team. That's why you share the early set. Once the new girl is hired, I'll have you working only three nights a week to lighten your load. When you feel you need time off, she'll cover for you."

Sydney felt a tap on her shoulder and turned around to find one of the young waiters.

"Syd, there's an urgent phone call for you."

She followed him to the back of the bar and picked up the red receiver on the counter.

"Sydney, it's Dottie. The burglar alarm is going off at the guest house."

"Oh, no."

"Peg and Max are on their way over to the club now. Peg's going to drop Brett and Max at your place and bring you here. The police should be here soon."

"Thanks, Dottie."

"I've been keeping an eye on the place for you. You've still got some stuff in there and you've been paying rent the whole time, so I've had timers installed for the outside lights."

"I appreciate that. I've been hanging on to the guest house in case Brett's landlord kicks us out, so we can have a backup plan."

"Someone must've been watching it and waiting for a chance to break in."

"There's nothing valuable there, anyway. Just some old kitchen stuff."

"Let's not forget Aunt Mildred's junky old furniture."

"I'm glad you took Tony's remaining furniture for the main house. I'll get Brett and we'll wait outside for Peggy and Maxine. Thanks for letting me know, Dottie."

"See you soon."

Her hands still trembling, she went backstage, where Brett was sitting on an old Windsor chair. Chuck was standing beside her, his orange satin shirt shimmering under the lights.

"Hon, you look pale as a ghost." Brett observed.

"Dottie just called. The burglar alarm went off at the guest house. Maxine and Peggy are coming to pick us up. Maxine's going home to stay with you and Peggy's taking me there to find out what's going on."

"I'm sorry, sweetheart. I'm just glad there was nothing of Tony's left behind."

"Me, too. It was clever that Dottie replaced all the leftover stuff of Mildred's with the rest of Tony's, so the guest house isn't sitting empty."

"Let's go and wait for the girls." Brett rose from her chair, "We can get our coats tomorrow."

"I'll get them for you and bring them to the house on my way home." Chuck offered, "Cleo won't mind getting them for me."

"Thanks, hon." Brett kissed his cheek.

* * *

She ran up the driveway, followed by Peggy.

"There she is, now. This is Sydney Goldstein." Dottie informed the officer.

"Hello, Ma'am." the young man approached her, "The front door's been forced open. I need you to go in and tell me if there's anything missing."

She complied in stupor. Gingerly stepping inside, she turned on the hallway light. On the wall in blood red, the words "Filthy Dyke" and "Muffe Diver" were spray painted. In the kitchen, barstools were knocked over and drawer contents were strewn about the floor. On the wall, "Sinner" and "Abombanatian" were spray painted in black. In the living room, a mid-century modern ceramic lamp was shattered. The empty dining room and the bedrooms appeared untouched. Hanging her head, she returned to the waiting officer in the hallway.

"Just vandalism. No theft." she murmured, "Looks like they fled before they had a chance to go through the bedrooms. The alarm must've scared them off."

"We've dusted for fingerprints around the door, in this area and the kitchen. Can you think of anyone who might have done this?"

"I don't know…I can't think of anyone."

"If you think of anything, let us know. I want you to know we take hate crimes seriously. We've apprehended the perpetrators who spray painted swastikas on the synagogue. We'll get these guys, too."

"Thank you." She smiled wearily.

"Why don't you re-set your security system and let us secure the place for you?"

"Of course." she punched in the code robotically and walked out into the night chill.

She provided contact information and answered more questions. Overcome by complete exhaustion, she sank on the front steps of the guest house, cold and numb.

"Sydney, let's all go in the house and have some tea." Dottie sat beside her.

"No, thanks, honey. I'd better get home. I don't want to tie up Peggy and Maxine any longer."

"It's okay. You don't have to worry about that." Peggy said.

"We're going to get together very soon and talk about all this – okay?" Dottie patted Sydney on the knee.

"Okay. Thanks, sweetheart." she smiled weakly.

Dottie accompanied them to Peggy's car.

"Take care. Call me if you need anything. I love you." she hugged her.

"I love you, too, Dottie." she kept an arm around her.

As she and Peggy drove away, Peggy honked the horn and they exchanged waves with Dottie.

"I'm sorry you had to go through this, Sydney."

"I should've been prepared for something like this. Those geniuses couldn't even spell half the hateful slurs they spray painted."

"There's too much bigotry and ignorance out there. It sickens me. I've never seen two people so deeply devoted to each other the way you and Brett are."

"Thank you, Peggy."

Back at home, the chamomile-scented warmth welcomed them. Faint strains of "You Go To My Head" could be heard from the phonograph.

"Sweetheart, I'm so glad you're back!" Brett, bundled up in a white thermal blanket on the sofa, beamed, "I hope they didn't cause too much damage."

"Nothing to worry about. The alarm obviously scared them off. How are you ladies doing?"

"We're having a splendid time. Maxine made a big pot of chamomile tea and she's been telling me all about her experiences working as a housekeeper at a haunted house in John's Bay back in the late sixties."

"I'll get you both some tea." Maxine offered.

"Not for me, thanks." Peggy said, "We'll head back when you're ready, Max."

"I'll be right with you as soon as I get Sydney's tea."

"Maxine, you don't have to do that. I can get my own." she protested, "You've both been so kind. Thank you." she hugged Maxine.

"Any time. I enjoyed myself immensely with Brett. I'm sorry about the vandalism."

"It's nothing major." she hugged Peggy, "Thank you for everything."

"You two take care of yourselves." Peggy said, "Good night."

"Sleep tight. Don't let the bedbugs bite." Maxine said.

"Good night, ladies. Maxine, dear, thanks for being great company." Brett called out.

"Sweet dreams." Sydney remained by the door and waved as they drove away.

"I missed you." Brett said when Sydney curled up beside her and kissed her cheek, "How were things back at the guest house? What damage did they do?"

"Just a broken old lamp and a few barstools knocked over. Forget about it. How are you feeling?"

"Quite rested."

"Can I get you anything?"

"Just yourself." she kissed her.

Sydney guided Brett's head to her chest and enclosed her in her arms.

"You know, when this dreaded curse takes over my body, I won't be able to do a lot of things."

"You never have to worry about that."

"I don't want to be a burden."

"You'd never be a burden. I feel honored to be a part of your life, to be able to do things for you."

"There's going to be a time when I won't be able to make love anymore."

"As long as I can hold you close like this, I am the happiest woman on earth. You're my world, Brett."

"And, you're mine."

"That's all that matters."

"Sydney...Thank you for loving me."

"I'm always going to love you, Brett." she kissed the top of her head, "Would you like to go up to bed?"

"Chuck's coming over after work with our coats."

"That's okay. He's got his own key and he knows what to do. He'll understand. I'll check things and turn things off down here first and then we can go up to bed."

She turned off the phonograph and checked the lock on the front door. Then, she went to the kitchen, where she could release the tears she had been holding back.

Chapter 8/ ALL THINGS THAT ARE BEAUTIFUL

"Someone's coming up the front steps." Sydney observed.

Brett strained her neck to catch a glimpse through the front window.

"Here comes trouble." she frowned, "That's Marty, the landlord."

"I'll handle him." she reassured her and opened the door.

"I'm here to see Brett." the gruff, middle-aged man scowled at her.

"Come in." she motioned him toward the living room.

"Hello, Marty." Brett greeted him cautiously, placing her newspaper on the side table and sitting up straight in her oversized armchair.

"Look, Brett, I'll get right to the point." he stood in front of her, "I'm giving you a month's notice to move out."

"Are you serious?" Sydney intercepted.

"You bet I'm serious. I've been flooded with calls from people in this neighborhood about homosexual activity going on in this house. I do not tolerate aberrant behavior. I'm a hard-working, church-going Christian man. I don't condone lewd acts against nature. You deviants are going to have to move."

"What grounds do these neighbors have for making such libellous claims?"

"They seen yous two kissing in front of your windows in clear view of people walking by."

"They are the deviants, if they are looking through people's windows. Voyeurism is against the law."

"Don't try to cloud the issue. Yous two are engaging in homosexual relations. That's enough grounds for eviction, as far as I'm concerned."

"And you think you can find a tenant as reliable as Brett?"

"This is a top-notch neighborhood. I can get the finest tenants."

"Sure. Great neighborhood. A bunch of Peeping Toms. Really classy. You'd be lucky to get university students or unemployed junkies who'd trash the place and burn it to the ground."

"That's enough. Shut your mouth. I don't have to stand here and listen to a castrating lesbo."

"Then, you can leave."

"I'm serious. Yous gotta be out by the end of the month."

"Nobody worth their salt is going to rent from you. The way you neglect your properties is well-known around the city. Brett didn't even have a bathroom from this century until 1984! Do you think any other tenant would've tolerated such substandard conditions?"

"You, shut your mouth, you!"

"Just admit it. You'll never be able to find another responsible tenant for this place unless you sink some cash into renovations. That kitchen hasn't been renovated since 1952."

"This is my house and I can do whatever I want with it. I can put it on the market and sell it for a hefty sum. You just watch me."

"You do that, pal."

"First, I gotta get yous lesbos outta here. Who's gonna buy a house of ill repute?"

"House of ill repute? This is not a brothel, Marty. Get your terminology straight." Brett laughed.

"Just clear out. I mean it!" he stormed out, slamming the door behind him.

"Sweetheart, you were terrific." Brett said.

"I'm going to make him an offer he can't refuse." Sydney winked, "You don't have to worry about that jerk anymore."

*　*　*

With bare hands, Brett nudged the soil lovingly around the base of the sapling, its trunk wobbly like a fawn's legs.

"There. Laurie's tree is planted." she lifted her hands out of the soil and gazed tenderly at the fragile tree; she looked proudly at the dirt embedded in the creases of her palms and under her short nails. "Soon, I'll be reunited with her. I wonder if she'll feel the same way about me."

"Laurie was a very troubled young woman." Sydney helped her up to her feet, "Most girls would give their eye teeth to have a mother like you." she picked up the gardening tools and led her to the garden shed.

Brett shuddered at the recollection of what had once transpired in that shed. She had chosen to withhold that from Sydney. Even now, the sound of the gunshot was never far from her nightmares.

"You know I'll always be there for Marin, Brettsy, and the boys, too." Sydney deposited the tools in the shed and locked the door.

"I know you will, and you'll do an amazing job. But I know, in time, Brettsy won't even remember me."

"Marin and I are going to see to it that Brettsy always remembers you." she led her to the back door with an arm around her.

"It's so nice not to worry about Marty anymore." Brett stepped out of her canvas loafers and into her jelly house shoes, "This house is ours now. No one can harass us."

"Those busybody neighbors can eat their hearts out. There's nothing they can do. We're not bothering anybody. They had no right to get Marty after us like that."

"He was more than happy to sell. You really scared him when you told him the only tenants he could get were students or junkies."

"All these beautiful heritage homes are going to wreck and ruin because the owners turn them into rooming houses or student housing for low rent. They fall into disrepair and get so dilapidated that they have to be demolished, or they burn down. People need to cherish these gems and make them into family homes."

"Thank you for rescuing our home, sweetheart. It's so nice to have Laurie's tree here, in our own yard." she washed her hands meticulously.

"Why don't you get comfy in the living room, honey? I'll make us some Earl Grey Tea."

"That would be heavenly."

"I'm going to find a dependable contractor and have a bathroom built on this floor." Sydney filled the tea kettle and plugged it in, "Peggy has some cousins in that line of work, so I'm going to get recommendations from her."

"It would be nice not to have to go upstairs every time we have to pee." Brett laughed.

"We can use the storage closet under the stairs and cut into the pantry. That should give us plenty of room for a three-quarter bath with a shower stall. It's next to the kitchen, so plumbing shouldn't be a problem. We can get rid of all the lead pipes and get some proper updated plumbing throughout the house, too, with some modern PVC pipes. Don't worry: I'll make sure there's very little disturbance or noise." she carried the tray into the living room and placed it on the coffee table; she poured tea into China cups with pansies.

"And, if you decide to sell somewhere down the road, you can get a better price, too."

"Oh, I'm not worried about that. Maybe we should update the wiring, too. Our old knob and tube is not exactly up to date. We'll get a two hundred amp entrance and an electric furnace. That old oil-burning monstrosity is costing a fortune to run, anyway. We'll have a cozy home that is safe to live in. I'll make sure they get at this very promptly, so they can be done before winter."

"Sweetheart, you are the most amazing woman. I feel so blessed. And, did I thank you enough for the wonderful housewarming party last weekend, sweetheart? Everyone showed up: Marin, Sam, Brettsy, Chuck, Dottie, Peggy, Maxine, and even the boys and Lisa made an appearance."

"Don't thank me, honey."

"They were all generous and brought so much food – according to our dietary restrictions, too. They made it such a special day for us."

"They all love you very much." Sydney said.

"Why don't you and I just take off?" Brett said, "Let's hop on a bus and go to Maine. It's so beautiful there this time of year."

"When do you want to leave?"

"The sooner the better. Bar Harbor's a lovely spot. I would love to see it again."

"I'll get on the phone to SMT first thing in the morning."

"I hope we can get a room at Bar Harbor Inn. It's such a gorgeous place. An ocean front resort. They even grow their own vegetables for the salads."

"I'll arrange everything. We also need to call your doctor and make sure you have enough meds for the trip."

"I can't wait."

"Do you want to take a nap while I prepare supper? I can put on some soft music."

"That would be nice, sweetheart." she placed her head on her favorite pillow and settled into a reclining position.

Sydney covered her with the blanket slung across the back of the sofa and kissed her forehead. She put on a Sarah Vaughan record on the phonograph and kept the volume low. In the kitchen, she removed the fresh greens and colorful vegetables from the crisper drawer and washed them under running cold water. Her tears fell freely down her cheeks.

*   *   *

Brett pressed Brettiella to her bosom and kissed the top of her head.

"Grandma! I missed you!" she wound her tiny arms around her waist.

"Grandma missed you so much, too!" she bent down to kiss her cheeks, "Heart of my heart, my beautiful angel."

"Where's Sydney?" Marin glanced around her.

"She's spending the afternoon with the girls, so you and I can have some alone time for a mother-daughter talk."

"She's always so considerate and caring."

"She's one in a million, my Sydney. I don't know what I did to deserve her."

"Mom, you deserve all things that are beautiful."

"All things that are beautiful: You, Brettsy, Sydney." she held her close.

"Brettsy and I can do some shopping for arts and crafts supplies at that store on Queen Street." Sam said, "Do you want us to pick up some McDonald's on the way home?"

"No need, Sam, dear. Sydney's prepared a feast for us: Pasta salad with all kinds of fresh veggies, a spinach feta pastry, and chicken breasts with orange glaze."

"Sounds scrumptious." he said, taking Brettiella's hand.

"Bye, Grandma!" Brettiella waved at her.

"See you soon, precious."

Brett and Marin waved at them from the living room window and sat on the sofa, hands linked.

"You look really good, Mom."

"Sydney takes good care of me."

"I'm so glad the two of you are together."

"And, here I was at first, worrying about whether or not you'd be able to accept it."

"Accept it? I'm ecstatic. I can't imagine any relationship as beautiful and fulfilling as the one you two have. So few women are fortunate enough to ever experience it."

"How many even admit they want it?"

"Oh, I do want it, but I also know I'll never get to experience it."

"Sweetheart...That is so sad."

"I am certain I'll never taste that much happiness in this lifetime, no matter how much I search for it."

"Oh, honey..."

"Hey, that's enough about me. We're here to talk about you."

"No, sweetheart. I want to know how you are. Is everything all right with you and Sam?"

"We're fine, Mom. We have a nice life as a family. But you can get buried under a conformist manure pile and can't keep up the plastic façade after a while. You carry on like a robot until your head explodes. Middle class respectability can be maddening. To have grand passion like yours is a remote, unreachable fantasy for women like me. Some of us are only meant to be in a cold, sterile, prudish, heterosexual existence."

"You never cease to amaze me with you sensitivity, my beautiful daughter." she embraced her, "I wish you could be happier. I hate to see you like this. I wish I knew what to do, what to tell you."

"Oh, Mom, don't worry about me."

"But I do. I love you so much."

"I love you. Thank you for being such a great mom."

Brett held her close, burying her face in her chest. When Sam returned later with Brettiella, he found them still huddled on the sofa.

Chapter 9/ MAYBE TOMORROW

Sydney produced an unsealed #10 envelope from the credenza drawer and handed it to Dottie.

"I'm glad you guys are going away. You really need the break." Dottie placed it on her lap, "Don't worry. Peggy's the best house-sitter in town."

"I'm not worried about that, sweetheart. Peggy's super responsible. God love her."

"She's perfect."

"I agree with you there. I'm worried about her safety."

"She's tough. She took self-defense classes. Nothing scares her."

"I know. But there's been some trouble here."

"What kind of trouble?"

"Our windows were getting egged on a regular basis."

"Juvenile delinquents! Somebody needs to slap them silly."

"Since we got the security system, it's been quieter. But they still shout obscenities when we're on the back deck or in the yard."

"Idiots. They need locking up."

"We were getting harassing phone calls multiple times a day until we changed to an unlisted number. I've been in contact with the officer who came to check the vandalism at the guest house and he's traced the numbers who called us. It was teenagers. He talked to their parents."

"This is so infuriating. You guys have enough troubles as it is."

"I try to protect Brett from it as much as possible. People in stores are pretty brutal, too. I've been followed by teenagers who've knocked grocery bags out of my hands and thrown rocks at me. Cars slow down when I'm walking home and men shout threats as they drive by. Some businesses even refuse to serve me. I don't tell Brett about any of it."

"Sydney, why didn't you tell me about all of this before?"

"I just try to ignore it. There's nothing I can do about it."

"Why can't they just leave you in peace?"

"They see us as a threat to the status quo."

"You know you can count on me, no matter what, don't you? No matter what you need, I'll do everything in my power to help."

"Thank you, Dottie. I'm very grateful."

"This envelope," Dottie held it up and observed it, "I guess it has all the information we need when you're away."

"It's got our itinerary, our room number, telephone number of the hotel, emergency numbers like Chuck and Keir. It also has the code for the security system, phone number for the alarm company, another house key, and the new unlisted phone number here."

"Thanks. I'll keep the spare key and the security code in the safe. I'll give the rest to Peggy. She has a photographic memory. She won't forget the code, so she doesn't need it written down." she placed the envelope in her handbag.

"Thank you so much for everything, Dottie. You guys are terrific."

"You're welcome. This is the least we can do. You go on and enjoy your trip without a care in the world. We'll hold down the fort."

"I appreciate that."

"God, how I detest this one horse hick town! I have a feeling I'm never going to be able to get out of here. I'm going to die here."

"Sweetheart, there's no way of knowing what the future holds."

"My parents keep telling me in all their letters that I should be either applying for grad work or law school here. I just don't think I'm cut out for it. Even if I could do the work, I'd either get bored and lose interest or I'd get super stressed out. I'm fine where I am. Office work is satisfying and pleasant. It doesn't consume me the way high profile careers would."

"You have to do what's right for you."

"I'm glad you had the chance to complete your degree in Toronto. Urban Sociology sounds so cool."

"Toronto feels like a lifetime ago. For me, it was a sanctuary. I wish I could move Brett there to keep her safe, to make everything better for her."

"You guys should go visit Eli and Daniel again."

"They're coming here next month. Maybe we'll go in the winter, if Brett's up to it."

"You two have the most romantic love story. That's what I want, some day."

"I hope you have it."

"Here I am, twenty-eight years old, married and divorced, and still uncertain about my future. I don't even know what my orientation is. I've had crushes on both men and women. So, what am I? What do I call myself?"

"Human." Sydney hugged her and kissed her cheek.

"Thank you. It took so much energy to hide part of myself from people and to overcompensate by expressing more interest in men than I actually had...It's like I had to present a man-crazy image, just so people would consider me acceptable. Crazy, isn't it? There were some girls in university who openly admitted to being bi, but they were always the super promiscuous, shallow girls. The sensitive ones must've hidden themselves away like me. Everybody my age treated me like a freakazoid. Nobody wanted to be anywhere near me. Guys wouldn't date me if their lives depended on it."

"Being sensitive in this callous world is not easy. I was all alone for fifteen years before I came to Beavertown. Men despised me. It's very hard for me to feel an attraction for either gender unless there's an emotional connection first...Of course, Warren was an exception." she winked.

"I'm like that, too."

"It's because we're sensitive. Sensitivity is a rare trait in human beings."

"Very rare trait. It's lonely being this way. I always wished I could be just ordinary, like other girls. They were so lucky. No matter how badly guys treated them, how much they rejected them, they kept chasing after them. They never felt hurt or humiliated or insecure. It's like they had no feelings. They went from one guy to another seamlessly. I can't be like that. If someone doesn't want to be with me or doesn't treat me properly, I'm done. And if I've been with someone and have split up, I can't just jump into another relationship the next day."

"That's the right way to be, Dottie. Sensitive people like us do not drift in and out of shallow relationships indiscriminately."

"Other people think there's something wrong with us if we don't party and sleep around. Everybody told me I must be mentally ill because I didn't sleep around."

"They did it to me, too. People don't get us, so they try to stigmatize us and ostracize us. But we are better than they are. We do our own thing and let others do theirs."

"Sometimes I get so sick of being alone. Being the invisible woman."

"We are lonelier. But in a different way. We don't need to fill a void with just anyone who comes along. We feel complete without being a couple. We want a deep connection and are willing to wait for it."

"I'll be waiting till I'm in a retirement home. My special someone must have a bad sense of direction and won't get here until I'm at death's door."

"Or it could happen tomorrow. You never know."

"Magical things don't happen to me, Sydney."

"J.T. did."

"Then, it ended."

"But you were happy while it lasted."

"He was very sweet and considerate. Honest and dependable. All that I wanted in a partner. And, then, poof! It was over."

"The fact that it ended doesn't make it less special. You'll always have beautiful memories."

"He started out calling me 'Doe' when we were dating, and later on, it became the more informal 'Dots'." she smiled wistfully, "I started out calling him 'Jack', but it felt weird and kind of incestuous, because of our Jack. His nickname was J.T., so I started calling him that instead. I do hope he finds happiness with someone nice and gets to have an old-fashioned family life. I couldn't be what he needed."

"You were both what the other one needed at that given moment in time."

"I love talking to you, Sydney. You always say the right things."

"We're kindred spirits. I know where you're coming from."

"There's something I've been wondering about: When someone is bisexual, do they feel equally attracted to men and women, or do they feel a stronger attraction to one?"

"It depends on the person. Sexuality is not a 50/50 split or an either/or. It's a continuum. The Kinsey Report is the only explanation that makes sense. Draw a straight line – excuse the pun. On one end, you have 100 percent hetero; on the other, 100 percent gay. No one falls precisely on one of those extremes. We are all somewhere in between. We are capable of a whole spectrum of emotions and relationships. Spirits have no gender. We love a person's soul regardless of their gender. False labels and false boundaries keep us all prisoners."

"Finally, something that makes sense! They brainwash us into believing it's wrong and sinful and deviant to feel things that are perfectly normal."

"They demonize those who are the most sensitive, most creative individuals in our society. Homophobia is a cancer. It eats a society from the inside and destroys everything in its path."

"No wonder so many nice people are so messed up."

"And, until Pierre Elliott Trudeau decriminalized it in January 1969, homosexuality was a crime. Probably still is, in some countries. His words are permanently etched in my brain."

Dottie joined her, as they recited in unison:

"There's no place for the state in the bedrooms of the nation."

"I really needed this talk, Sydney." Dottie hugged her, "I don't have to deny a part of myself anymore, just to feel accepted. Even if I never find the opportunity to live the life I want, just acknowledging it to myself provides inner peace. I can accept myself as I am and hold my head up high."

"Sweetheart." Sydney pressed her close, her tears falling on Dottie's hair, "You should always hold your head up high."

"Sydney, you're the best." Dottie wiped away her own tears with her left thumb as Sydney released her.

"So are you."

"I should get going. Brett and Chuck are probably going to be back from visiting Maggie pretty soon, anyway."

"We're keeping Maggie in the dark about Brett's condition."

"She wouldn't be able to handle it."

"Definitely not. We couldn't do that to her."

"She must be relieved that you bought the house from that cranky old goat. Especially with all her stuff still in the guest house."

"When she went into the care home, she gave Brett access to her bank account, so she could keep paying her rent for the guest house. Deep down, a part of her had to be hoping she'd be able to return some day."

"She's leaving everything to her only remaining family member, isn't she? Her cousin from Philly or some place."

"She gave some things to Brett before she left, but the rest goes to her cousin."

"Does she know that you guys are...you know?"

"She does." Sydney smiled, "And, she's very supportive. She joked with me that she had been carrying a torch for Brett and she was jealous of me. Bless her heart."

"She's quite a lady." Dottie walked toward the door, "Please give my best to Brett and Chuck."

"I will." Sydney hugged her, "And you take care of yourself – hear?"

"You, too. I'll make sure Peggy gets the stuff." she patted her handbag.

"Thanks, honey."

Sydney stood on the front porch, watching Dottie become smaller as she walked down Smythe Street until she was a blue dot on the horizon.

Chapter 10/ SOMEWHERE

"I can't wait to have a humungous lobster dinner, sweetheart!" Brett turned away from their second floor turret window overlooking the ocean.

Hanging up their garments from the day, Sydney smiled and winked at her. She wondered if Brett had been to this resort with Tony at some point during their long relationship. They rarely spoke of him, and when they did, it was with the nostalgic fondness one feels for a long-lost friend. She wondered, looking down at them now, what he would be feeling about two of the women he had once loved being lovers. Somehow, she sensed he was happy for them and was watching over them. Tears escaped from the corners of her eyes. She blinked them away.

"Do I look okay, hon?" Brett was twirling like a young ballerina in her dusty rose chiffon cocktail dress.

"Like a beautiful summer rose." she gazed at her in longing.

"What are you wearing, my darling?" she held her shoulders.

Still in her cream Antron teddy, Sydney trembled under her touch. She wanted to take her to bed immediately and feel her, warm and alive in her arms.

"I'll wear whatever you want me to."

"How about the champagne silk dress? You look scrumptious in it."

Brett sat by the window watching Sydney dress.

"Why don't we go to Camden next week and stay at the Victorian Windward House? From there we can go on to

Bennington, Vermont, and stay at the Paradise Motor Inn. It has the cutest flagstone patio and geometrical swimming pool...Then, from there, we can go to New York."

"Are you sure you're up for all this, hon?" Sydney frowned in solicitude.

"Yes! Yes! I feel so energized being with you. I could dance the night away with you and not even care what kind of reaction we get from people!"

"We can do anything you want." she twirled around, the circle skirt of her dress blossoming like an enormous morning glory trumpet.

"You look breath-taking, sweetheart." Brett sighed.

Maintaining a socially acceptable distance from each other, they strolled down the crystal-lit hallway, descended the majestic staircase to the rose-colored circular dining room with the chandeliers. Encapsulated by the timeless enchantment of this elegant hotel, revelling in the splendor of a gracious by-gone era, they rejoiced in the exhilaration of their love for one another.

*   *   *

Brett leaned back on her white plastic lounge chair and placed her tall, tropical virgin cocktail on the plastic poolside table beside her. Enormous brown sunglasses concealed her face.

"This motel is aptly named." she said, "This place is paradise."

"I feel honored to be in your home state. Vermont is so beautiful."

Reclining in a prone position on the lounge chair beside her, Sydney lowered her own sunglasses.

"We've been on the road for over three weeks, but it just seems like a few days." Brett said, "We leave for New York tomorrow...Autumn in New York. We'll be there to see it."

Sydney reached out to squeeze her hand. The sparse architectural design of the motel reflected the modernism of the past three decades. Nestled in a wooded, secluded area, it was a complete escape from the drudgery of the mundane. Brett sipped her sunny orange drink and twirled the fuchsia parasol attached to the pineapple wedge.

"I love that little gift shop they've got here." she popped the pineapple into her mouth, "Do you mind going back there for another look-see, hon?"

"Sure." Sydney rose and took Brett's hands in her own to gently pull her to her feet. With one hand on Sydney's elbow for support, Brett tucked both of their paper parasols into her pocketbook, along with their cocktail napkins. Sydney admired the fluid movement of Brett's long, strapless floral print sundress in vibrant magenta, lush green and jonquil. Brett paused to scratch a mosquito bite on her calf. Sunlight danced on the brightly-colored leather straps of her sandals that matched the colors of her dress. The bland song that had been audible through the aged outdoor speakers ended abruptly and Barbra Streisand's voice paralyzed them with her tender rendition of "Somewhere". It was their song, Brett had told her, and sung it just for her at the club. Even now, standing so close beside her on the cracked concrete, she ached deeply for her.

And, that night, when Brett came to her in chocolate satin, she felt that deep ache acutely. The summer was nearly over. The leaves were turning. September in New York would soon melt into October. She would witness firsthand, the beauty of the city Brett held so dear and Ella Fitzgerald sang about. The summer had been theirs. But summer was a short season.

Chapter 11/ FOR THE LOVE OF BRETT

"Edna, dear, how are things with you and Sid in Toronto?" the voice on the other end spewed out a saccharine greeting.

"Annette?"

"Yes, dear. It's me, your sister."

"How are you and Donald?" Edna asked with measured caution.

"We love it here in Florida. We don't miss New Brunswick at all."

"I'm happy for you."

"I mean, who is there left back there now? Just Dottie and Warren. Even most of our friends are all here in Florida...Oh, Edna, dear, I know I haven't been very nice to you...I apologize for blaming you for the things your daughter has done."

Sid wheeled himself into the room and looked quizzically at his wife. Edna shook her head in exasperation, covered the mouthpiece with her hand and whispered:

"It's Annette."

His eyes widened in disbelief. Both of them rolled their eyes.

"I hope Toronto agrees with you, dear." Annette continued, "It's also a good thing you have some distance between you and your daughter."

"Our daughter has a name, you know."

"Well, of course...I didn't mean..."

"We would've preferred not to have so much distance between us, but we're able to make things work."

"That is so nice for you, Edna, dear. I'm afraid things are not as good for us."

"What's wrong? I just spoke to Dottie yesterday and she sounded fine."

"It's not her. It's Garrett."

"Garrett? I thought you'd lost touch with him years ago."

"He's dead, Edna."

Edna wanted to feel some sort of grief for her nephew, however, was unable to call it up from within her. She silently asked God for forgiveness.

"How did it happen?"

"The obvious way. He overdosed on heroin. Died in a back alley in Los Angeles. He had been homeless for a very long time, they said, and well-known to the authorities there...All these years of not knowing where he was, and now, this. Where did we go wrong, Edna? We messed up with both of our children."

"Dottie's perfectly delightful." Edna protested, "You couldn't ask for a better daughter."

"Don't get me started on Dorothy, dear. She's a lost cause."

Edna shook her head and exchanged glances with Sid.

"Both of us have been disappointed by our children, sister, dear."

"Both Sid and I happen to be very proud of our Sydney."

"Really, Edna." Annette snickered, "Even as lazy and unmotivated as Dorothy is, at least, she's not a lesbian."

"Sydney's happier now than she's ever been. Her happiness is the only thing that matters to us."

"Of course, dear. You tell yourself that. She's quite the vixen, that daughter of yours. She seduced all three single Horncastle men, and then it turns out she never even liked men, after all. She was only after the money and prestige."

"You know very well she was in love with both Jack and Tony, and felt attracted to Warren."

"She certainly fooled a lot of people into believing that, didn't she? Now, the cat is out of the bag. It just goes to show, you never can tell who the lesbians are. Both of them are very attractive women. Nothing mannish about either one...Ooo, look at the time. I must go now, Edna, dear. I'm still in a state of disbelief about Garrett, you know."

"I'm sorry for your loss, Annette."

"Thank you, dear. Well, I've got to go now. Bye."

Edna hung up the phone and sighed deeply. Sid wheeled himself closer to her.

"I think I was better off when she wasn't on speaking terms with me."

"It's very sad what closed-mindedness can do to destroy relationships. You two were as close as sisters can be. Then, she sided with Don's family against our daughter and turned on you."

"Donald was your best friend for years and he turned his back on you, too."

"He chose his family. She should have chosen her own family, as well." he took her hands in his own.

"My sister knows what side her bread's buttered." she squeezed both of his hands.

"That family's put Sydney through so much."

"May God forgive me for saying this, but, I'm pleased Audrey, Willard and Mildred are gone. And Annette and Donald are far away. I remember something Sydney once said: 'The Horncastles eat their own young.'."

"Very astute."

"Your family's treated me far better than my own sister and my other siblings ever did. Living here has been a breath of fresh air."

"We're free from that toxic family and our daughter has finally found the love that always eluded her."

"I wish they could've had many years together…I wish they could've become a couple from the beginning, instead of running away from their feelings…Now, they have less than a year left. I know they are going to make every second of every day special, live each day as though it's their last."

"She's really going to need our love and support when Brett's gone." he said.

"She'll have us, Ethel and Ira, Eli and Dan to nurture her. We are blessed to have such a sensitive, loving daughter."

"I wouldn't trade our humble life for the Horncastles' for anything in the world. We have far more riches than they could ever imagine."

"I love you, Sidney Goldstein."

"I love you, Edna Goldstein."

* * *

The knock on the door was tentative. She took the unsealed manila envelope from the top of the writing desk and opened the door. They were both grinning broadly. She stepped out to the hallway and closed the door behind her.

"Is she sleeping?" Eli asked.

"Just drifted off a few minutes ago."

"She must be exhausted. We've been all over today." Daniel said.

"I'm glad we had the chance to visit all the places that are special to her. Physically, it depleted her, but, psychologically, she's in a very good place."

"You must be pretty tired yourself."

"I'll be fine after a good night's sleep. It's exciting to explore New York. The three of you are very familiar with it, but I'm just discovering it."

"Weren't you here on your honeymoon with Tony?"

"I don't think she saw anything except their hotel room." Eli winked at Daniel.

"We saw a play and went to a greasy spoon afterwards, but, yes, the rest of the week, we didn't leave our room." she blushed and squirmed uncomfortably.

"We have some good news." Eli, whose hands had been behind his back the entire time, handed her a sheet of paper with an address and a book of stamps.

"You've got the address!"

"I told you I would." he winked, "And there are enough American stamps for the self-addressed envelope to be mailed to Canada."

"Thank you so much!" she kissed his cheek, "This is going to be the best surprise ever!"

"You go to our room with Dan and get it ready to mail. I'll stay with Brett in case she wakes up and needs something. We'll mail it as soon as you've got it ready."

"Thank you, thank you." she beamed, "This is so important for her."

"Let's just hope she hears back." Daniel led her down the hall as Eli tiptoed into the room where Brett slept in total oblivion.

Chapter 12/ HOW DO YOU KEEP THE MUSIC PLAYING?

"Jack, you've been in a funk for months now." Aydin sat beside him on the sofa.

"It happens to all of us." Kent reassured him.

"Every single time? With every partner?"

"Maybe you're getting too stressed out about it. Just concentrate on the lady and how much you desire her."

"It's so demoralizing. I give up."

"There are other ways to pleasure your partner." Aydin winked.

"Women have certain expectations." Jack said.

"Then, you've been meeting the wrong women, my friend."

"It was so much easier and more spontaneous with Stephen. He was more understanding."

"But you didn't have feelings for him."

"I don't for any of the women I've been trying to date, either. I don't even think it's a gender thing. I had a complete connection with only one woman. There was always something lacking with the others – even Cicely and Ellie. Perhaps, I can have that elusive connection with a man, as well. I mean, if the emotional connection is there, the rest should follow."

"Jack, you're deep, man." Aydin patted his knee.

"It makes sense to me." Kent said.

"You know what this means, right?" Aydin said, "You're coming to Mark's party with us on Friday night. You might meet your Prince Charming there."

"Even if you don't meet he right guy there, hopefully, you'll relax and enjoy yourself, Jack." Kent said.

* * *

"We had such a lovely Christmas, didn't we, sweetheart?" Brett said brightly.

"It was good to have your brothers and sisters here with us for the holidays." Sydney placed the wash basin on the portable table beside the bed and deftly removed Brett's lacy cotton gown.

"They came to say their final good-byes." Brett's smile was almost ethereal, her eyes transfixed on something beyond her.

Sydney sponged her with meticulous care in delicate strokes of the lavender washcloth, as though soap and water could eradicate every trace of cancer from Brett's body. Loose skin was hanging from Brett's arms and legs like tattered rice paper lampshades. Her abdomen caved in like a deflated parachute. She wrapped her in a soft pink towel and dried her off gently, taking care to protect her fragile skin. She smoothed on the cream recommended by the visiting nurse, to prevent bed sores, now that Brett was confined to bed. She also needed to be turned over regularly. Fragile and weightless under her touch, Brett felt more like a porcelain doll. As she removed the towel from Brett's emaciated body, Sydney was struck aware of the fury with which this insidious disease was devouring Brett's flesh. She was losing her. She was losing her to that most heinous of all adversaries.

She dressed her in a blue flannelette gown and placed additional pillows behind her. She turned on the television set to the music channel. Keir and Toby had set up the T.V. in the bedroom, though the cable company had been less than reliable in the installation of the second cable outlet, failing to show up at scheduled times, not having the required equipment once there, and rescheduling yet again. They had since taken up following soap operas – the only alternative to mind-numbing daytime talk shows.

Sydney stretched out beside her and nuzzled into her. Brett still loved to cuddle. Though their once vigorous lovemaking was now a thing of the past, they still enjoyed a tender intimacy: Sydney massaged her; they kissed, caressed, and held one another. When Brett expressed the need, Sydney provided her with release. Most often, Brett was unable to reciprocate, though she eagerly attempted to do so. The love in her eyes was all Sydney needed to feel satiated.

Brett now required daily bed baths and the frequent use of a bed pan. She took all of her meals in bed. Groceries were delivered to the back door. Maxine came in once a week to perform household chores. When Sydney needed to leave the house on rare occasions to pay bills, she did so on the days Maxine was there. On days when she was able to leave her other house cleaning jobs early after completing her required work, Maxine came by to cook for them. Judy, the middle-aged extramural nurse fulfilled her obligatory visits with uncanny punctuality. She maintained a cool reserve around them at all times. Sydney wondered if that was simply a professional veneer, or disapproval of them.

"Look, sweetheart, channel 2 has brought back reruns of 'To Tell The Truth'!" Brett said, scanning the weekly television guide, "I really missed that show! I love their theme song, too. It's on at four. What if I fall asleep and miss it?"

"You won't miss it." Sydney winked mischievously.

Brett looked at her quizzically.

"I have a surprise for you." she pointed to the VCR under the cable box, "Keir hooked it up yesterday when you were sleeping. Now, I can tape shows for you to watch whenever you want."

"I didn't even notice it. What a wonderful treat! But, sweetheart, those video machines are so expensive."

"Keir got us a deal on it. He has a friend at the electronics store."

"Thank you, sweetheart."

"I'll make you some lunch, honey. Will you be all right till then?"

"You don't have to worry about me, hon. I'm like a kid in a candy store with this new gizmo. I'm going to pick out all the shows we can record on it."

Sydney kissed her cheek and descended the stairs slowly. Her knees ached; her chest felt tight; her own body felt like excess baggage. Through the window in the foyer, she observed diamond-encrusted snowflakes falling in a playful dance. She opened the front door to check the oversized mailbox. A familiar manila envelope with the smoothed out crease down the middle addressed to Brett in Sydney's own handwriting peeked out at her. She retrieved it, ran back inside, and shut the door behind her. In the dining room, she opened a credenza drawer and produced the silver frame she had bought for this occasion. Deftly opening the envelope, she slid out the 8 x 10 black and white glossy of the sultry, doe-eyed woman and placed it securely in the frame.

"Mail for Ms. Brett Morrow!" she announced, running up the stairs, and burst into the bedroom, holding up the framed photo.

"Brett Somers!" Brett lit up like a megawatt floodlight, holding out her hands like a child waiting for candy, "How did you do it?"

"I had some help. When we were in New York, Eli found the address through some of his contacts, and bought sufficient American stamps for the self-addressed envelope I enclosed. I wrote her a letter and told her all about you. Then, Eli and Dan mailed it from New York."

"Sweetheart, thank you so much! I can't believe it! Brett Somers sent me her autographed photo! She even inscribed it to me! My namesake now knows I exist!" she clutched it to her bosom and kissed it.

"Where would you like it, sweetheart?"

"Right here, on the nightstand, hon, so I can look at her all day."

Sydney placed it beside the bejeweled lamp.

"People have been kind to us." Brett mused, "Everyone's been so caring and helpful...Maxine, Peg, Dottie, Chuck, Eli, Dan...Even Warren: He supervised the workers during the renovations while we were away and made sure it was all done according to our specifications. We came home to an orderly house with all the work completed. It was very kind of him."

"We are blessed to have such caring friends." Sydney caressed her cheek.

Like a fawn who had not yet grown into her enormous eyes, Brett's face bore a waiflike innocence. Her skin was nearly transparent. Her hair was cropped short and no longer dyed to its original brown. She glowed with such inner beauty, Sydney's heart skipped a beat.

"Stay here with me, sweetheart." Brett pleaded, "Never mind about lunch."

Sydney slid beside her and snuggled up with her.

"I need to feel close to you." Brett placed her head on her breast, "I'm sorry if I'm needy."

"Never." she kissed the top of her fragrant head, "You could never be needy."

Brett was slipping away from her. Day by day, she was growing weaker.

"If I'm still here by Easter," Brett said, "I'd like to give a little party for Brettsy."

"You'll be here for a long time past Easter." Sydney stroked her arm, "And, I'm sure she'd love that. I'll take care of the arrangements."

"Why don't we invite the two little girls down the street? She likes playing with them when she stays over with us."

"We'll have a brightly-colored cake with bunny decorations on top. I'll get hats and party favors."

"I hope the Spencers allow the girls to come to the party."

"They've always allowed them to come here to play with Brettsy, so, I don't think it should be a problem, but I'll go have a talk with Rachel and Sabrina's mother and invite her to come along as well, if she wishes."

"Thank you, sweetheart."

Sydney caressed Brett's silken strands of silver hair.

"Marin and Sam have bought a bigger house in a better school district." Brett said, "I was thinking, maybe they could get some movers and take the stuff that is going to them, anyway. All the boxes are marked and the pieces of furniture are stipulated in my will. There's a copy in the filing cabinet and Marin has a copy, as well. This way, it will be over and done with, and you won't have to deal with the upheaval after I'm gone. The boys already have their stuff at their respective homes. This way, the only items remaining here will be what belongs to you and you won't have to deal with all the commotion."

"You're always so thoughtful." Sydney took her hand and kissed it.

"You're so thoughtful and loving with me." Brett said, "Do you have any idea how much I love you?"

"My beautiful Brett...This love of ours has no bounds." Sydney's fingertips traced the curve of Brett's slender neck.

She wished life had a rewind button; she wished they could return to that glorious day in the spring of 1976...

......"I'll introduce you to your co-worker." she remembered Tony leading her down the stairs to the dressing room on her first day of work at Chandler's Lounge.

She remembered hearing her voice for the first time, from behind the door after Tony's knock.

"Come in."

Tony opened the door, and, there she was, in all her splendor.

"Meet our new singer, Sydney."

"Hello." her smile was radiant, "I'm Brett." she shook her hand, "Very pleased to meet you."

“I’m Sydney.”

“Brett’s going to show you the ropes.” Tony said.

Tongue-tied, and quivering, Sydney could feel the sun rising after a long and sleepless night...

If only she could rewind life to that moment, she would hold on to Brett and never let her go.

“Why don’t we play a record and just stay here?” Brett said, “I’m not even hungry yet.”

“I’ll play any record you like.” Sydney slid off the bed and crossed the room to the stereo.

“Tony Bennett would be nice.”

“Tony Bennett it is, then.”

Once the record began to play, Sydney resumed her former position beside Brett. So many years had been wasted running from their own hearts and denying their feelings for each other. They had been robbed of the memories they could have created, the love they could have lavished on each other.

Tony Bennett was singing ‘How Do You Keep The Music Playing?’. Sydney’s tears fell on Brett’s hair. How long would she be able to keep the music playing?

Chapter 13/ DIDN'T WE ALMOST HAVE IT ALL?

Waiting for Brett's lunch to warm up in the oven, she stood by the kitchen window. Spring showers had washed away all traces of the stubborn brown-speckled snow. This was the warmest April in years. Crocuses were peeking playfully in purple, yellow and white. On a sudden impulse, she took the strong shears from the utility drawer, and ran outside to gather a small bouquet. She returned to the kitchen to arrange the tender flowers in a green jam jar filled with water. The oven timer went off. She removed Brett's lunch and spooned the brown rice and vegetable casserole on to the plate with the daisy border. She covered the plate with a pink mesh food umbrella. She was well aware that Brett was eating all of her meals only to please her despite her ever-waning appetite. Upstairs, she placed the bamboo tray across Brett's lap. Brett's eyes lit up to see her.

"Crocuses! Thank you, sweetheart! They're so cheery and bright."

"I wanted you to enjoy them. I'll pick more and bring them up with every meal."

"You're so good to me." Brett blew her a kiss and opened the pink dome. "Everything looks so good. The rice and veggies, the pineapple juice, green tea, fresh grapes."

"I hope it tastes okay."

"Everything you make is delicious, hon." Brett smiled, "Crocuses herald the arrival of spring. When I see my first crocus of the year, I know winter's behind us."

"This winter went by so quickly."

"When you try to savor each day you have left, it slips away even faster."

Brett made an effort to eat every morsel of food Sydney had prepared.

"I'm glad Brettsy had fun with her little friends and the weather was mild enough to play in the yard. But I know you were all tuckered out that day. I'm sorry about the toll everything is taking on you, sweetheart."

"That's not important. All I care about is making you happy, Brett. I just want to be with you."

"Oh, my darling." Brett's eyes were brimming with tears.

Sydney placed the tray on the hall table and stretched out beside Brett. She remembered lying on the narrow bed at Daisy's house, with Brett's small, firm breasts pressing against her back and sending jolts of electricity through her. She remembered feeling sticky, contaminated, and ashamed, aware of Warren's scent mingled with her own. Brett's warm body beside her felt warm, safe, blissful.

"What are you thinking about, sweetheart?" Brett asked, "You're deep in thought."

"I was thinking about the night you stayed with me at Daisy's house."

"Following your passionate encounter with Warren?" she laughed softly.

"Except, Warren was the farthest thing from my mind. My heart was crying out for you."

"So was mine. But I couldn't mess up your life like that. You were so vulnerable."

"I was so terrified of alienating you if I let you know how I felt. I thought that you'd reject me and I couldn't risk losing your friendship."

"I thought I might scare you off, too. I wanted to take care of you and protect you."

"And you were amazing. You were always there for me. Brett, I wasn't alive until I met you."

"And, I didn't know what love was until I met you." she took Sydney's hand in hers and pressed it to her cheek.

"Would you like some music?"

"That would be lovely, hon."

"Any requests?"

"No. You choose."

She selected a Sarah Vaughan album, set the volume low and returned to her spot beside Brett.

"Beautiful choice." Brett placed her head on Sydney's left breast and let her arm rest across her abdomen. Sydney's right arm encircled her. They remained that way and listened to the jazz diva.

When "You Go To My Head" came on, Brett's tears fell uncontrollably. Sydney caressed her softly. Brett soon drifted off to sleep. Sydney watched her chest move rhythmically with each breath. Lately, she found herself checking to be certain Brett was still breathing each time she fell asleep.

The phonograph shut itself off with a click. Its red light continued glowing in the darkened room like a lit cigarette. In the silence, she could hear the sound of Brett's breathing. She cradled her. Her chest against her own, she lay listening to that precious sound – a sound she would not be able to listen to for much longer.

* * *

Those eyelashes, still long, fluttered, and her eyelids parted slightly.

"Sydney?"

"I'm here, sweetheart." she squeezed her hand.

"How long have I been sleeping?"

"About four hours." her fingers brushed away strands of hair from Brett's face.

"I can't believe I made it to summer. It's your love and care that made it possible. I love you so much, Sydney."

"I love you more than life itself, Brett."

"How do I let you go?"

"You don't have to. You can let me go with you."

"My darling." Brett's gnarled fingers rested in Sydney's hair, "I promise you I'll never leave your side. I'll stay close and watch over you as you live your life. When we're eventually reunited on the other side, nothing and no one is going to be able to tear us apart."

"I want to go with you now. There's nothing for me here. I have no reason to stay behind."

"But, you will have a reason some day. You just have to trust that there's a greater plan and a reason that you're here."

Sydney held her close and inhaled the scent of her skin.

"Why don't we go out and get some sun and fresh air?" Brett suggested, "It's a beautiful summer day."

"That's a wonderful idea."

In late spring, they had set up a makeshift bedroom in the dining room with a wicker room divider to separate it from the living room. The credenza, table and chairs were moved to Keir's old room and his queen size bed, nightstands and chest of drawers brought down. A wheelchair ramp was installed on the front porch.

Sydney dressed Brett in a cool cotton sundress with a lavender print. She brought her wheelchair from the back corner of the room and eased her into it. The white floppy sun hat and oversized sunglasses completed the ensemble. A water bottle tucked under her arm, Sydney led her slowly down the ramp to the small patch of green in front of their house. She sat beside her on the red wooden lawn chair. The notoriously oppressive Beavertown heat was in full force.

"Are you all right in this heat, sweetheart?" Sydney asked in solicitude, "It's 87 degrees."

"It doesn't bother me, hon. I'm making the most of this lovely weather while I can."

"Why don't you have some water?" she handed her the bottle, which Brett accepted eagerly.

"Lovely day, isn't it?" a young woman in athletic attire walking by smiled at them.

"Yes it is." Sydney smiled back.

Brett smiled and waved. The trees in the park were resplendent in every vibrant shade of green. Children's carefree laughter was heard from the wading pool.

"It's a glorious day to be alive." Brett's eyes appeared to be turned heavenward.

A monarch butterfly landed on Brett's shoulder and remained there.

In the evening, Sydney set up the small bistro table on the back porch for their meal, brought out the green salad, the watercress sandwiches and the lemon Perrier.

The cable company had been called upon to install a third outlet in the dining room and the T.V. and VCR had been moved down from the bedroom. Sydney settled Brett in bed while she cleaned up in the kitchen. In the background, she could hear Brett's laughter as she watched her beloved namesake on reruns of "Match Game". A new channel had been added two weeks earlier, featuring this vintage game show. She joined her when she heard the familiar theme song heralding the conclusion of the program. Brett turned off the television with the remote and sighed.

"Is there anything you need, sweetheart?"

"All I need is you, my darling...Lie with me, Sydney. I need to feel you close..."

Sydney turned on the radio to the FM channel, lay beside her and placed Brett's head in the crook of her arm. The scent of fresh roses filled the room. With Brett's heart beating against her own ribcage, and the warm air from her nostrils on her own face, she could, for this moment, convince herself that she could shield Brett from the inevitable.

Then, the heartbeat and the warm breath were no more.

"Brett, honey, please wake up!" she pleaded, "Brett, please wake up...Brett, don't leave me!" she held her tighter, "Don't leave me, please!" she kissed her face feverishly.

On the radio, Whitney Houston was singing "Didn't We Almost Have It All?"

It was hours later, when Chuck and Maxine knocked and received no response that Chuck opened the door with his key. They found Sydney clinging to Brett's lifeless body. Maxine nudged her gently.

"Sydney?"

"Honey, it's time to let her go." Chuck said gently.

"No." she pulled Brett closer.

"Sydney, please come with me." Maxine pleaded as Chuck attempted to pry her loose.

"Brett needs me. I'm going to stay here with her."

"Honey, she's gone."

"No. She's not gone. She's just asleep. I want to be here when she wakes up."

"She's not going to wake up, dear." he attempted to pry her away again.

"Sydney, please let me take care of you." Maxine reached out to embrace her.

"I can't leave Brett. She needs me."

"She's all right now. She wants you to go with Maxine." Chuck said.

She reluctantly released her hold on Brett and kissed her forehead.

"I love you." she whispered.

Maxine led her away to the back porch, keeping an arm around her as the torrent of tears overwhelmed Sydney.

*   *   *

She sat in the center pew of the front row, with Edna and Sid on each side of her. His wheelchair was in the aisle beside her, and he clasped her hand. Marin and Sam, Toby, Keir and Lisa were seated to Edna's left, with Maggie at the end of the pew. Leonard and Greeney were directly behind Maggie. Maxine, Peggy and Dottie were in the center, with Dan, Eli and Chuck behind Sydney. In the third row, Warren sat behind Chuck. Josh, Gene, the bandleader, and Johnny O. occupied the rest of the third row. All the past and present employees of the club were in the rows behind them. The first two rows on each end were filled with Brett's siblings, their spouses and children.

Edna studied Sydney's solemn face: Her sunken cheeks, her pallor, her listless eyes framed by dark circles. Her salt and pepper frizzy hair was tied back haphazardly in a low ponytail. Edna stroked her back.

"We are here to celebrate the life of Bernadette Morrow, or "Brett", as she was affectionately called by those close to her." the bespectacled middle-aged minister began, however, Sydney was unable to process what was being spoken.

"And now, her two best friends are going to perform two of Brett's favorite songs: The wartime classics by Jerome Kern: 'Long Ago And Far Away' and 'All The Things You Are'. Charles Seabrook on the piano and Sydney Goldstein, vocals."

Chuck nudged her gently.

"Syd, we have to go up now, dear."

She rose robotically. Her dad moved his wheelchair to make room for her to join Chuck in the aisle. Chuck guided her with a hand on her elbow. As she sang, she felt a pair of hands on her shoulders. She was able to maintain her composure and complete the songs.

"Now, Brett's friend Sydney Goldstein is going to say a few words about her." the minister announced.

Sydney clutched the edges of the podium.

"Brett was my best friend, my life companion, and the light of my life. Her loss leaves a void that can never be filled. We had very little time together before cancer took her away from me. She was the most extraordinary human being I have known. She was the most loyal, most caring friend one could ever hope for. If you had Brett for a friend, you had a treasure. She would sacrifice her own happiness for those she cared about. She would gladly give up her time for those in need. It's difficult to imagine no longer seeing that beautiful smile of hers lighting up a room. Brett's love was unconditional and knew no bounds. She was gracious and compassionate, even toward those who were unkind to her." she dabbed at her eyes and paused to regain her composure.

Chuck, who had remained in the background, offered her a glass of water. Reassuring him with a smile that she had composed herself sufficiently, she returned to the podium:

"Brett's great passion was music, and she brought immeasurable happiness to others through her singing. She was an inspiration to all who knew her. I feel I have been truly blessed for having her in my life. Now, she's singing with the angels."

Overcome with tears, she ran back to her seat. Edna placed her arm around her and Sid rested his hand on her elbow.

Chuck approached the podium:

"My cherished friend Brett leaves behind three children and a beloved granddaughter, Brettiella. Brett's daughter Marin will now say a few words." he nodded to the pale Marin, who was coming up the aisle. She took her place beside him shakily, clearing her throat.

"I didn't know my mom until I was an adult. At the hospital where I was born, there was a mistake and I went home with the wrong parents. My mother was given their baby, who was seriously ill. She doted on that little girl. Following numerous operations and hospitalizations, Martha Evelyn passed away three years later. Mom had always suspected she had been given the wrong baby, though the hospital denied it vehemently. She knew the sick baby needed her and she gave her all her love and attention. For years, she kept searching relentlessly for the real Martha Evelyn. She never gave up. Mom moved here from New York with her second husband and their three children in 1966. I met her when I was in university and we became close friends. I moved into her house as a lodger and spent my best years there with her, Keir, and Toby, though at the time I didn't know they were my brothers. In 1976, she learned through her private detective that I was Martha Evelyn. We were reunited after twenty-six years. She has been the mother all girls dream of having. I had so little time with her, but what I had was golden. I miss her deeply. My daughter is very young, but she has cherished memories of her time with her grandmother, and I intend to make sure that my mom's memory is kept fresh in her mind."

Following Keir, Toby, and Maggie's tributes, Chuck returned to the podium:

"Brett and I were friends and colleagues for over twenty-five years. We went through a great deal together. She was a true friend, the genuine article. All of us who were fortunate enough to be among her friends were truly blessed. We are better for having known her. If she's looking down at us now, she's probably trying to come up with a way to make us laugh." his misty eyes scanned the solemn faces, "Each one of us has many humorous anecdotes about her to comfort us. We miss you, dear friend."

"And, now, Mr. Seabrook and Miss Goldstein are going to sing two other selections." the minister took the podium as Chuck accompanied Sydney back, "The first one is 'Somewhere' from West Side Story, and the other one is a Barry Manilow song: 'I Made It Through The Rain'."

As she sang, Sydney's tears flowed freely. She felt soft kisses on her forehead and kept going.

During the graveside service, she wept in Edna's arms. As Brett's casket was lowered, she broke free and attempted to throw herself on top of her. Chuck and Keir pulled her away.

Throughout the reception back at the church, she forced herself to smile and shake hands.

"Why don't you come stay at Dottie's with us, darling?" Edna whispered to her on their way to Chuck's car.

"It's okay, Mom. I'd rather go home."

"Then, let me stay with you."

"No, it really is okay. I'll be fine by myself."

"I don't think you should be alone, dear."

"You don't have to worry about me, honestly."

"I really don't think it's a good idea for you to go into that house by yourself."

"Please, Mom. I really need to be alone tonight. I'll feel closer to Brett. I can't deal with any type of interaction now."

"Promise you won't do anything foolish?"

"Don't worry. Brett won't let me."

Toby helped her dad out of his wheelchair and into Chuck's back seat. He folded up the wheelchair and put it in the trunk.

"I've got to go now. We'll talk first thing in the morning." Sydney said, "I'm getting a ride with Peggy again, so Toby can go with you and help Dad." she kissed her cheek.

"I love you, sweetheart."

"I love you, too, Mom." she leaned into the back seat to kiss Sid's cheek, "I love you, Dad."

"I love you, sweetheart." he kissed her forehead.

"Thank you, Chuck." she hugged him.

"We'll talk tomorrow. Take care of yourself." he kissed her cheek.

"Thank you for everything, Toby." she hugged him.

"Take care, Syd."

She waved at them on her way to Peggy's car. Dottie and Maxine were in the back seat. She slid in beside Peggy.

"Do you want to come out to the house and stay with us, Sydney?" Dottie asked.

"It's very kind of you to ask, but no thank you, sweetheart. I'm just going to go home."

"Would you like one of us to stay with you?" Maxine offered.

"It's okay, Maxine. I'll be fine. Thanks for asking."

"If you change your mind, just phone, and I'll come pick you up." Peggy said.

"Thank you. I appreciate your offer, Peggy."

The three of them observed her opening her front door with her key and turning around to wave at them. They waved back and drove off.

The house was damp and dingy. The scent of roses still lingered in the air. She removed all of her clothing in the makeshift bedroom, and once she freshened up in the bathroom, she slipped into one of Brett's nightgowns. She lay on the wrinkled bedsheet, untouched since that day, and inhaled the moist scent of Brett's body on the faded cotton. A pair of arms cradled her through the long and sleepless night.

Chapter 14/ I'LL NEVER STOP LOVING YOU

The sheets were freshly laundered, new covers and bedspread placed meticulously, as though it were an ordinary day. Maxine had removed all the dead flowers, dusted the wood furniture, vacuumed the rug and even scrubbed the bathroom. Every trace of death had been eradicated, every surface sanitized. Sydney stood before the open closet door, inhaling the scent of Brett's skin. She removed the dresses, the blouses and sweaters one by one, held them up, and smelled them. The delicate scent of "White Shoulders" perfume permeated the entire closet with barely a tinge of "Soft And Dri" deodorant. The natural scent of Brett's own flesh mingled with the fragrance created that unique "Brett" scent. She pressed each garment against her cheek and hung it back up again in precisely the same spot. Shutting the closet door, she crossed the room to Brett's antique cherry vanity table and picked up the silver brush she had brushed Brett's hair with every morning. A tangled nest of silver clung to the bristles. She picked at several strands with her fingertips, welcoming the sting of the harsh nylon bristles. Curling the silver threads around her index finger, she squeezed them into the unoccupied section of her locket opposite Brett's photograph. She touched her index finger, first to her lips, then, to the photo, and closed the locket, tracing its heart-shaped outline. She sat on the ecru eyelet ruffled vanity chair. A smile came to her lips at the sight of a smiling Brett peeking through the antique silver frame in the corner of the vanity. The two of them were standing with arms around each other's waists. She held it close for further scrutiny. An elderly couple from Arizona, staying at their motel, had taken it for them in Bennington, Vermont, in front of the pool. Brett was fawn-like in beige jersey. She placed it back beside the green round box of dusting powder. In the opposite corner, beside the peach abalone lamp, was an Art Deco silver frame, housing the photograph she treasured most: The one she had taken of Brett on a picturesque deserted stretch of beach in Maine somewhere, between their many destinations, a little place whose name she could not recall. In a white gauze diaphanous dress and white picture hat, she possessed an other-worldliness, walking away from the camera toward the horizon, tilting her head to the side just so, to smile back at her...Saying goodbye at the end of her journey.

"Why did you have to leave me, Brett?"

Then, the torrent came. A subtle touch on her shoulder, a kiss on her cheek comforted her. Her head buried in her hands, she sobbed shamelessly. The hand remained on her shoulder. She longed to go to sleep and never awaken. Never awaken to this darkness. Yes, just go to sleep. The tortured strains of "Round Midnight" kept playing over and over in her mind.

*　*　*

Playful fingers of dawn creeping through the crack in the curtains, taunted her. Her head a complete vacuum, she awoke to discover she was still alive. Her heart still continued beating, still continued stinging, still continued aching. The inevitable stared her cruelly in the face. There would be countless days like this. She had endless hours, endless days, weeks, months, even years ahead without her. It might be best to end it all now. She could just walk away from this and be with Brett. Without her, there could be no life, no meaning. Wrapping an oversized burgundy pile robe around herself, she went downstairs. She opened all the drapes in the living room and dining room to allow the sunlight to frolic through the house. In the chilling silence, she crept from empty room to empty room. As she stood caressing the piano keys, a wave of comfort swept over her.

* * *

"Chuck, I'm going to miss you!" she flung her arms around his neck and kissed his cheek.

"I'm going to miss you, too, sweetheart. We've been through an awful lot together."

"Please don't forget to write."

"You, too."

"I hope you'll be happy in Vancouver."

"Now that my uncle in John's Bay is gone, there's no reason left for me to stay around here just to get kicked in the teeth by local yahoos."

"Take care of yourself."

"You, too, Sydney." he kissed her moist cheek.

She watched him going through the security check and turning back to wave at her. Yet another goodbye. She knew Chuck would never want to return, even for a brief visit, to the bitter memories of Beavertown. She waved in slow motion from behind the glass, as the frail, aging man boarded his plane and waved for the final time. Another loved one was being taken away.

* * *

The woman with the large midriff, dressed in black stretch pants and a dark green shapeless tunic had the appearance of an overgrown watermelon. Her ear-length black-dyed hair was cut in the shape of a globe. Her fierce hazel eyes swept the room in disdain.

115

"Junk. Nothing but junk. Isn't it just like Cousin Maggie to live like a hobo? She was always eccentric, but, this is ridiculous! With all her money, you'd think she'd have bought some nice stuff! Nothing but gaudy thrift shop clothes, dusty old books, and tacky costume jewellery!"

"She had the antiques. They're already shipped out to our place." the white-haired man in the loose brown trousers by the window reminded her.

"Hideous old things! Monstrosities!"

"At least, we can sell them and make money off them."

"I suppose you're right. They must be worth a pretty penny." she smirked.

"Let's just hurry up and get all this trash sorted through." the man stood, surveying the piles on the floor, his hands sunk deeply in his pockets, "Pack 'em up for the Sally Ann."

"Stanley, you never know what treasures she might've stashed away around this place. She was such an odd duck. Her mother's ruby brooches could be wrapped in flea market scarves."

"She sure was an odd one, that Maggie."

"Look at all these boxes of photographs from the seventies and eighties! They're of people we don't even know."

"Chuck it all out, Carol. Knowing Maggie, all her friends must've been a bunch of oddballs and misfits, too."

"Such a flaming shame. Her husband left her a tidy sum. And she just lived in squalor all those years."

"Maybe she gave away all the valuable stuff and left the worthless junk for you to go scavenging around in. She did have a warped sense of humor."

"I know. She wasn't exactly peachy-keen about me, either. If I weren't her last surviving relative, there wouldn't have been anything for me."

"Yeah – even so, she still left all her money to science."

"At least, we've got the antiques."

"I'd like to get an early start, Carol. It's a long drive back to Springfield."

"I'm almost done. Stanley, look: This picture frame looks like sterling silver."

He moved closer for a look.

"Sure does."

Carol carelessly removed the black and white photograph from the frame and placed the frame in the tan overnight bag beside her. She threw the photo into the cardboard box labelled "Tomatoes", which was overflowing with discarded objects from the cramped apartment.

"We're done." she grinned in self-satisfaction, "Stanley, dear, can you take the flight bag to the car? The landlady said to leave the Sally Ann stuff here. I reckon she wants to rummage through it first and pick out what she likes. Oh, Stan, dear, can you put this last box of trash out on the curb?"

"It's all piled up. The box won't close."

"It's all right. Tomorrow's collection day, anyway, the landlady said."

"Yes, dear." he shook his head and lifted the carry-on bag, "Light as a feather."

"It's pathetic that this is all we can use. The rest is junk. I'll take one last look around the place, to make sure we didn't miss anything nice."

"Sure, dear." he took the open box of refuse, "See you in the car."

Carol gave the forlorn residence a final walk-through, deposited the key in the top kitchen drawer, as Sydney had requested, and locked the door behind her.

Their green sedan pulled away in a cloud of dark exhaust fumes. The open tomato box sat on the curb among more weathered, torn but closed companions, its contents exposed. The red and gold tinsel Christmas tree garlands, paperback recipe books, chocolate boxes, cat ornaments from the Five And Ten…and a 6 x 12 black and white photo of Brett in a black evening gown at the top.

* * *

"Rachel, wait up!" Sabrina called out, running after her sister, her brightly-colored hair ribbons swinging behind her.

"Come on, slowpoke!" Rachel laughed and stopped at the corner to wait for her.

Behind her, the wind had picked up the photo at the top of the box. It fluttered away and landed on the sidewalk amidst fallen maple leaves.

"Come on!" Rachel called out again.

Sabrina caught up to her, breathlessly, her thin ribbons trailing behind in bands of fuchsia and grape. She bent forward from her waist in an attempt to alleviate the pain she was experiencing from running.

"You're such a wuss." Rachel giggled, playing with her sister's French braids.

"Rachel, look!" Sabrina pointed at the ground by her feet.

"I don't see anything."

"Look now!" she brushed away the leaves obscuring the photo.

"That's Brettsy's grandma!"

"Why is it here?" Sabrina picked it up and straightened her back, "She was a beautiful lady."

"Why don't we give it to Miss Goldstein? It must've been thrown away from Mrs. Cheeseman's place by her relatives." Rachel wiped the surface of the photograph deftly with her fuchsia glove.

The girls skipped playfully down the street. Across the way, Wilmot Park was resplendent in crimson and gold, with all the maple trees dancing in wild abandon like gypsy women.

Part Two

Chapter 15/ RASPBERRY DANISH

He was face to face with the most extraordinary pair of eyes he had ever seen: A translucent amber, the eyes of a savage beast. And, in that moment, he could no longer feel the water running down his face from his rain-soaked hair. He attempted to thank the stranger holding the door for him, but was unable to find his voice.

"It's pretty nasty out there. I'm glad you didn't get soaked." the younger man broke into a smile.

"Th...Thank you." he stammered.

"I saw you from the window."

"Foolish of me to forget my umbrella."

"Join the club. I'm the most forgetful person, ever." the young man giggled nervously.

"I used to carry an umbrella on days like this, but I kept forgetting so many of them on subways that I decided to take my chances with the weather."

"Sounds just like me. Can I buy you a hot drink to warm you up? Cappuccino, if I'm not mistaken?"

"Why, yes, of course. But, how...?"

"I was behind you a couple of times when you were ordering. And a banana muffin, am I right?"

"You have an amazing memory."

"I've been observing you here these last couple of months: You always get a cappuccino and a banana muffin, and take that seat at the small table in the back. You're deep in thought. Sometimes, you jot things down in a small notebook."

"You're very observant."

"You're friends with Aydin Sayer and his partner Ken Something-Or-Another, aren't you?"

"Yes, I am. It's Kent. Kent Dogan. I haven't seen you at any of the parties."

"Oh, but I've seen you." he smirked, "I'm Laurence, by the way."

"Jack." he extended his hand.

"I know." he shook it and held onto it, subtly caressing it, "I know who you are, Jack. I've wanted to meet you for a very long time."

Jack studied the handsome man with the shock of black curls falling around his face. The intense gaze in those entrancing eyes were piercing through him, sending shivers down his spine. The knowing smile on Laurence's face told him he was aware of Jack's admiration. Jack followed him sheepishly to the counter. His head was spinning. Laurence ordered their cappuccinos, a banana muffin for Jack and a raspberry danish for himself. He took the drinks and led the way to his table by the window. Jack followed him with the small plates. As Laurence placed the drinks on the table, his hand brushed against Jack's softly. To conceal the shaking of his hands, Jack kept them on his lap. He had lost his appetite. Laurence's savage eyes scrutinized him with keen interest. His lips curled in delight as Jack gripped his coffee cup with both hands and spilled a little on his shirt.

"My place isn't far from here." Laurence said, "The rain has finally let up. We can walk over there, if you like."

Jack could not feel his legs when he rose from his chair. As he stumbled, Laurence reached out to steady him. He walked alongside Laurence, feeling trapped in an alternate reality from which there was no escape. Yet, something was compelling him to allow this to unfold. Despite attending all the parties and social events with Aydin and Kent and being approached by a multitude of desirable men, he had been unable to bring himself to take things this far. They walked two or three blocks in some direction. He knew he would never be able to retrace their steps later if required to do so. Nothing about this maze of identical streets and rows upon rows of red brick tenements felt real to him. He followed Laurence blindly into one of the nondescript buildings. The front entry smelled of urine and vomit. They scurried up the two flights of well-worn, curving stairs with the ornate iron railing. Laurence stopped before one of the wooden doors with chipping dark brown paint and produced a skeleton key from his pocket. The only source of illumination in the hallway was an ancient frosted white ceiling fixture with a single light bulb. The overwhelming smell of cabbage and garlic made him gag. This building was still a step or two above his days on Skid Row.

"Nervous?" Laurence stood aside and motioned to him to enter the dingy space ahead of him.

Trembling in trepidation, Jack stepped inside tentatively. Laurence closed the door behind him.

"Don't mind the minimalist décor." Laurence remarked, aware of his baffled expression.

"It's...It's quite hip, actually." Jack reassured him, "Very modern...vibrant."

Though sparsely furnished with second hand furniture, the apartment possessed a harmony of sorts...a threadbare burgundy afghan covering the faded, stained cumbersome Colonial sofa with a navy and brown indiscernible print...the green milk crates holding record albums, the cable bobbin side tables, tasselled lamps with green satin shades, a fuchsia and gold striped semi sheer fabric haphazardly covering the window...The scuffed and paint-splattered hardwood floors were bare.

"A struggling actor can't afford anything nice, but I know better days are ahead of me."

"I like your choice of colors." Jack said feebly.

"Don't be nervous, Jack." Laurence took his hand, "You've been with a man before. You and Stephen Browne were quite an item at one time."

Yes, but, he had known Stephen before, even if he did not remember him, he thought. There had been an instinctive familiarity, a level of comfort with Stephen that he did not have with other men.

The kiss took him by storm. Laurence's tongue tasted like coffee and raspberry danish.

"Ooo, you taste so good, Jack. Exactly the way I always imagined."

It was too late to back out now. Laurence's lips moved lower, to his neck, while his fingers urgently unbuttoned his shirt and caressed his chest. He kissed him again, his raspberry-infused tongue dancing seductively around his teeth. Jack moaned. Laurence took his hand and led him down the corridor to the bedroom.

* * *

He awakened to shouting from a neighboring apartment. Beside him, Laurence was sleeping, his mouth trumpeting like an obscure flower. Jack slipped out of bed and gathered his clothes from the heap at the foot of the bed. He dressed in the living room, checked his pockets for his keys and wallet, and examined the contents of his wallet. Then, he let himself out without a sound.

A disheveled, stale-smelling man brushed past him on the stairs. A white-haired woman on the main floor with an abundant bosom dressed in an ill-fitting faded orange print shift dress was sweeping the aging brown linoleum outside her apartment. She eyed him with suspicion. An image of a young slender woman with long red hair in an orange shift dress flashed before him...a woman with a serpent's green eyes and a menacing laugh...The same woman he had remembered momentarily under hypnosis...the one with the acid tongue...He scurried out to the street. If he only knew what direction to take. He wondered if the old woman suspected he had been there for a sexual encounter. Was this building known for such indiscretions? He turned right for no particular reason, other than to get away swiftly.

He quickened his steps when he heard his name being called behind him. There was no hope for an escape now.

"Jack, why did you take off like that? I thought what happened last night was special for you, too. I thought it meant something to you."

"It's just that, I...Casual sex is not really my thing...No offence. Don't take it the wrong way. I had a lovely time. It just felt...wrong."

"You sure didn't act like you felt that way last night."

"I got caught up in the moment."

"Swept away by passion, you mean."

"It's just that...I need to get to know someone first...establish a bond."

"It's not like we were strangers. We were giving each other the eye for weeks at the coffee shop."

"Don't get me wrong. I find you very attractive. It just seemed...too sudden, too fast."

"Do you want to start from scratch and take things slow, then?"

"Yes, I would like that." he smiled with a sigh of relief.

"Hello. I'm Laurence." he extended his hand with a devilish gleam in his eye.

"I'm Jack." he shook it, suppressing his laughter, "Pleased to meet you."

"Would you like to grab some breakfast together?"

"I would love to."

"Good. Now that we've got that out of the way, we can find a nice quiet place to become better acquainted."

Jack followed him into a trendy coffee shop for the younger crowd. They ordered gourmet coffee and designer breakfast sandwiches. Laurence selected a small round table by the window.

"So, what's your story, Jack? Someone noticed me checking you out at one of the parties and told me you were like a big pop star or something. Is that true?"

"In another lifetime." Jack looked away, focusing on the strangers on the sidewalk, "Long, long ago."

"Wow. I thought Eric was pulling my leg. He also said you had a dozen ex-wives. Is that true?"

"A dozen is an exaggeration, but, yes, I've been told there have been several marriages in my past."

"Quite the ladies' man." Laurence smirked.

"Not really. Apparently, none of them worked out, except one."

"Then, why did you divorce her, too? Was it just a force of habit by then?"

"That, I'm afraid, is a very long story."

"I've got lots of time."

"I think it's best saved for another time." he blinked away his tears, "What about you?"

"I'm an aspiring artist and actor waiting for my big break. I'm from a huge family and I have Romani heritage on my mother's side."

"That's fascinating." Jack studied Laurence's long fingers picking at his sandwich.

The raging storm in his brain was subsiding. For the first time in years, all was well in his world.

Chapter 16/ A LESSON IN LITERATURE

The tall, pudgy man with the prominent chin at the front of the room twirled his moustache.

"Why did Caleb want to return to Nova Scotia to live on the family farm after his brother died?...Sarah?" he nodded toward an apathetic young woman in the second row.

She shrugged her shoulders.

"Does anyone know?" he searched faces around the room, "Ms. Goldstein?"

"Because he's a character in a Canadian novel and he has to do everything possible to make the novel as dull as possible." she responded wearily.

Laughter erupted.

"I would like to hear more." the man smirked, "This is quite interesting, Ms. Goldstein. Can you shed more light on that remark, please?"

"Canadian Literature is lacklustre and predictable." she said, "The plot is either flat and mundane or bizarre and morbid. The landscape is bleak and the characters are shallow and soulless."

"Hey, she's right, man!" a young man shouted from the back of the room.

"Why do we have to read this boring crap, anyway?" another young man called out.

"And, how do you feel Canadian Literature could become more appealing?" the man kept his gaze focused on Sydney.

"I would like to see more diversity…Characters with more depth and substance. I'm sick of one-dimensional female characters who engage in casual sex with every man they meet, and male characters who are macho slobs. I would like plots dealing with a wider variety of human experiences. I would like to see a higher calibre of people being represented."

"This is very interesting, Ms. Goldstein. Your perspective is quite amusing. You're very blunt. I suspect you step on quite a few toes."

Self-conscious laughter was heard from the back of the room.

"You seem to be put off by the very things other people find stimulating. Goody Two Shoes characters are boring. Villains are much more fun to read about."

"Villains are dull and predictable."

"I suspect you've been quite Americanized by your friends and associates over the years. American Literature is full of repulsive 'nice' characters and sentimental drivel."

"American writers know how to create well-rounded, complex characters and original plots. They know how to strike a balance."

"I suppose purple prose is very appealing to females." he smirked.

"You have your opinion and I have mine."

"That's all for today, class." he looked away from her, "I'm having a party at my home this weekend. You're all invited. Even you, Ms. Goldstein. It starts on Saturday at four. There'll be unlimited pizza and beer, and I have a sauna. It's 123 Windsor Street. See you all on Saturday."

Sydney gathered her books hastily and walked out to the corridor, unaware of the professor's eyes taking in the view of her buttocks as she swept past him. She noticed a familiar face in the hallway and smiled in acknowledgment.

"Hi, Sydney." the slender young woman approached her, "I think you are right about Canadian Literature. I don't like this prof at all."

"Other English profs are no better, Olga." Sydney said.

"I think I've made a mistake in choosing English as my major."

"If you're not too far along, you can change your major."

"This is my second year."

"It shouldn't be a problem to change it at this point, then. Do you have anything else in mind?"

"Maybe history."

"Why don't you discuss all your options with your faculty advisor? You shouldn't remain stuck in something you don't enjoy."

"I chose it because I want to be a writer, but I'm finding creating literature is the opposite of studying existing literature."

"Studying literature stifles creativity, especially when the profs are as obnoxious as the characters in the novels."

"They seem to be...overly confident, rude..."

"You're being too kind. They're pompous, callous, condescending assholes."

"I love the way you insult people!" Olga beamed.

"Thank you." she laughed, "When you get to be my age, you call 'em as you see 'em."

"This prof, Dr. MacMillan, I think he has...how you say, 'the heat for you'."

"He doesn't have the hots for me, Olga. He's a sexual predator and he thinks I have easy virtue."

"Easy virtue?" she appeared puzzled, "What that means?"

"He considers me a woman with loose morals." she explained.

"How can he think that about a nice lady like you?"

"Olga, dear, I'm not anybody's idea of a nice lady."

"I don't understand."

"You haven't lived in Beavertown long enough to hear all the stories."

"I told my parents I have made friends with a nice lady in this class and they are very pleased. At first, they didn't want me to take an evening class, but they were so happy when they found out there's a responsible adult in this class, not just wild teenagers. My parents are very strict."

"If they heard any of the local gossip, they'd be scandalized to think their daughter was consorting with the likes of me."

"I can't imagine people saying bad things about you." she held the heavy door open for her as they stepped outside to the November chill, "Which way are you going?"

"To the SUB."

"SUB? What is SUB? Isn't that a sandwich?"

"Yes, it's a sandwich, but the Student Union Building is called SUB for short." she smiled.

"Oh, I see. I'm going there, too. My dad's picking me up there. He can drive you home, too, if you like."

"No, thank you. It's very kind of you, Olga, but I have a ride home."

"With a boyfriend?"

"No no." she laughed, "Three friends. One is my cousin. She's a legal assistant. Her best friend is a paralegal. They are studying French because the law firm they work for is now providing bilingual services. The third friend has a cake decorating business and she's studying French as more of a personal interest."

"What about you? You didn't want to study French with your friends?"

"I'm half French, and I lived in Montreal for a considerable amount of time, so I'm fully bilingual."

"Lucky you."

"Yes, lucky me. Auditing a course with Chester MacMillan."

"Auditing: Do you still need it for a credit?"

"Heavens, no. I wouldn't want to be in that position at my age. I have a degree in Sociology and have no desire to put myself through the torture of meeting deadlines and writing exams at this stage in my life. Do you think I'd be mouthing off like that in class if I needed that guy's blessing?"

"It sounds so nice, having an evening out with your friends. I'm not allowed to go out with friends. My culture is very restrictive, so my parents are overprotective. We've been in Canada for five years now."

"You're over eighteen, Olga, so you're an adult, and you're free to do as you please."

"They say, until I have a job and pay my own way, I am still a child, and must abide by their rules. But it's not easy to find a job. I had a bad experience two years ago. I worked in a boutique. My boss was a mean lady who told lies about me and blamed me for something that wasn't my fault, so I couldn't get another job. By the time I found out she was badmouthing me, I had lost out on a lot of jobs."

"Don't give another thought to that nasty woman. Just live your life and be happy."

"Thank you. Where are you meeting your friends?"

"In the coffee shop. Their class runs later. Some night, if your parents are okay with it, would you like to join us for a 'girls night out' after class? We usually grab a bite at The Admiral afterwards. Your dad wouldn't have to come out in the evening. We can drop you off at home afterwards. Peggy has a van with plenty of seating."

"That's very nice of you. But I live on Argyle Street. Is that out of the way?"

"Not at all. That's not far from where I live, on Odell Avenue. I'll give you my number." she produced a small notepad and a pen from the outside compartment of her pocket book and scribbled with a flourish, "The first is my home number, and the second is the number for the music shop: Goldstein's."

"Thank you. I'm sure it'll be okay with my parents. I have to meet Dad on the other side of the building, one floor up. Thank you, Sydney."

"You're welcome, Olga. Hope to see you next week." she waved as Olga climbed the stairs.

In the coffee shop, the jukebox was playing Jon Secada's "Forever's As Long As It Takes". She approached the counter and ordered black tea from the smiling young man in the white uniform.

Chapter 17/ ANGELS' DAY OFF

"Nurse! Nurse!" he roared.

"Yes, Mr. Horncastle?" a flustered middle-aged nurse burst into the room.

"I want my dinner!"

"The dietary department is going to be bringing up the dinner trays any time now, sir."

"I'm ravenous! Can't a person get any co-operation around here? Can't you see, I'm stuck here in this bed!"

"Sir, we're doing the best we can."

"Where's that cute blonde nurse, Denise? She promised she'd feed me tonight. I don't want Big Agatha feeding me again. She's too rough."

"Mr. Horncastle, please be patient. Everything's under control."

"Where's Nicole?"

"Is that your niece?"

"No! My niece is Dorothy. Nicole's my travelling companion. She was with me when I had the accident. She was the one who called for help when I hit that tree."

"No, sir. It was a Marcus Collins who called for help. My sister is a 911 operator and she took the call."

"Where's Nikki? Has she been here; has she called asking about me?"

"No, sir. No one named Nicole's been in or has been in contact by telephone."

He scoffed and broke into uncontrollable laughter.

"Your niece has been contacted and she's on her way here. Dinner won't be too long now." she slipped out.

Alone in the darkened room, he shut his eyes and felt himself freefalling into an abyss.

* * *

The thud of her own skull being smashed against the floor echoed in her ears. She felt her life force fading, draining away from her, a strange darkness descending upon her. She could hear them scurrying away like rodents. She fought with all she had to remain conscious...She fought in vain, fully aware of her fate...So, this was how it was all meant to come to an end...No, she could not...would not accept that...If she could just crawl as far as the door, perhaps a passerby would notice something was amiss...If she could just crawl as far as the door...Then, it all went dark...

* * *

Olga wept inconsolably in Greeney's arms. Greeney stroked her back with maternal care.

"She shouldn't have been working alone on a Friday night. I should've stayed after my shift ended."

"There's absolutely nothing you could've done, dear. You would've been lying in the next bed in the same condition. There's never been a robbery at Goldstein's in all the years it's been in business. And, it's been around for a very long time. Sydney's grandfather was the first owner. I worked for him, back in the day, too. Don't do this to yourself, dear. You did what anyone would've done – left after your shift was over."

"I took the deposit to the bank when Sydney came in, so, there wouldn't have been any money in the cash register."

"It must've been teenaged punks looking for drug money. I can't believe what the world is coming to. I'm going to make some calls Monday morning to have some surveillance cameras installed." she shook her head, "I never could've imagined it would come to this."

"They beat her up so badly." Olga wept, "Is she really going to be all right?"

"She's going to need a lot of rest. It'll be a while before she's able to get back on her feet, but they're very optimistic she'll make a full recovery."

"I'm going to make sure she does."

"You're a sweetheart, Olga."

"She gave me a job when no one else would. She was so patient with me when I made mistakes. When Maude quit, she could've hired another older lady, but she took a chance on me."

"Sydney is an incredibly kind and generous lady...a real treasure. She's the best friend and colleague you could ever ask for."

"Has Sydney owned this store for very long?"

"The last seven years. Her father sold it to my husband several years before that, but when Sydney's partner passed away, he offered to sell her back the business. At that time, she was finally in a position to buy it back. After all, it had been 'Goldstein's' for so long before Len changed it to 'Greene's Records'. Sydney kept me on as manager. She, Dottie and Peggy also bought back the club from us and returned it to the way it had been originally, with a jazz lounge and a restaurant."

"You mean 'Jack's Place'?"

"Yes. Her late husband left her well provided for."

"Is that Jack Chandler?"

"No, dear. Tony Horncastle. Jack Chandler is still alive, somewhere, with no memory of his life here."

"That is so sad."

"You must have heard that she also lost her partner, Brett Morrow."

"Yes, I did. It's so tragic the way she died."

"Brett was loved dearly by all of us. My Len bought the building from Tony Horncastle shortly after it was rebuilt. Back in the seventies, it was a white Mid Century Modern building called 'Willow Place' with 'Chandler's Lounge' and 'The Castle'."

"Why was it rebuilt?"

"It was destroyed in a devastating fire."

"Oh no. That's terrible."

"That's when Jack Chandler was initially presumed dead, then discovered to be the victim of a nefarious plot. Sydney was critically injured; she nearly didn't pull through. She and Tony rebuilt the place from scratch."

"That is quite a story. Poor Sydney's been through so much. Who's going to be taking care of the club while she's laid up here? Dottie's been in Colorado since her uncle's skiing accident. Peggy's got a heavy work schedule at the office doing both her and Dottie's jobs."

"Cleo Johnson, the manager, is quite a capable lady, and Peggy's just a phone call away. Also, Eli and Daniel always lend a hand. They're regulars there and look out for Sydney and the girls."

"That's a relief."

"Now, Olga, dear, from now on, you and Maxine are strictly on day shifts. No Thursday or Friday evenings. What days are good for you? I know Friday is usually not a good day for you."

"That Friday, my classes were all exam reviews, so I took the day shift when Kirk got sick. Tuesday and Thursday are the best days for me. I have only one class in the morning on those days, so I'm free by noon."

"Tuesday and Thursday afternoons for you, then." Greeney pulled out a brown leather-bound notebook from her pocketbook and wrote swiftly with the Schaeffer pen she produced from an inner compartment. "I'll give Maxine Monday and Wednesday. Sydney and I usually have alternating Saturday mornings. We pop in and fill in when needed. I'll cover Saturdays. Kirk usually works Thursday evening and all day Friday. I'm going to make sure he's the only one to work evenings. No more cutting him slack and giving him a night off just because he's my nephew."

"I hope they catch the lowlife boys who did this to Sydney."

"I'm hoping the surveillance cameras from the jewellery store next door caught them."

"I hope so, too. It must've been all of Sydney's angels' day off."

"Let's pray they're back on the job, dear." she patted her shoulder, "I'm going down to the cafeteria to get some coffee. Would you like some?"

"Yes, thank you. That's very kind of you."

"Hang in there, honey. I'll be back soon." Greeney walked out toward the elevators, remembering another night long ago when Sydney had been assaulted at the shop. Funny how circumstances could change so drastically with time and forgiveness.

* * *

"That Stanley girl sure has bad luck, Hilda." Helen glanced at her companion across the orange table in the cramped coffee shop.

"She sure does. Somebody should write a book about her."

"That's a darn good idea. It sure would be a juicy one."

"Our town is goin' to hell in a handbasket, dear. A robbery! Who robs a music store?"

"It's drug addicts. Drugs are destroyin' the world. Soon, we won't be safe walkin' down the street in broad daylight."

"Sure thing, Helen, dear."

"Who do you reckon she'll be shackin' up with next?"

"My money's on Warren Horncastle – her old flame. Now that they're both banged up, they'd make a good pair." she cackled.

"You've got a point there!" Helen squawked, "They can have matchin' hospital beds in their bedroom!"

"You're a hoot, Helen! They're sayin' he may never walk again, you know. I hear he's sellin' his red Miata. I wish I could afford it."

"We can go halfsies on it and use it every other day. You can have it Monday, Wednesday and Friday. I'll have it Tuesday, Thursday and Saturday. We'll let the boys drive it on Sundays."

"You're dreamin' in Technicolor, dear. We could never afford it, halfsies, threesies, or foursies."

They laughed uncontrollably, unaware of the strangers' eyes observing them with hostility.

"I can't believe all them people are gone, Hilda. The whole Horncastle clan. And, Stanley's parents."
"It sure don't seem real."

"Dorothy and Warren are the only Horncastles left. When they're gone, that'll be the end of the Horncastles, seein' as neither one has any young'uns."

"Sad, ain't it? All that money gone…"

"I heard it all went to Stanley. Tony Horncastle got mad at his parents and funneled the family fortune into her account."

"She destroyed that family, Hilda."

"Can't say I'm too sad about that. She done more good with it than them people ever did."

"Can't argue with you there, dear."

"Them people at that table are starin' at us, Helen. Why don't we get goin' and check out that sale at The Bargain Store?"

"Good idea."

The patrons at nearby tables scrutinized them as they put on their coats and walked out of the coffee shop, abandoning their empty cardboard cups and soiled napkins at the table.

Chapter 18/ A DAY IN THE LIFE OF A FOOL

Jack bolted up in bed, overcome by a sense of impending doom. Unable to breathe, he peeled off the white duvet cover and sprang to his feet. Laurence was sleeping perfectly unaware, his smooth brown shoulder illuminated by the streetlight. He moaned and reached instinctively for Jack; unaware of his absence, he turned over and continued sleeping. Jack tiptoed out of the bedroom. The champagne glasses from last night's Valentine celebration were still on the cable spool table. The red foil garlands and the red and gray balloons clashed with the bohemian décor. He stood by the window and lifted the hippie style improvised curtain. For a city that never slept, it was eerily silent for Valentine's Day. That inexplicable sense of foreboding engulfed him and shook his body.

"Jack..." a tender whisper in his ear made the hairs on the nape of his neck stand on end. He felt a gossamer kiss on his cheek.

"Sydney?"

"Goodbye, Jack." she whispered.

"Sydney...Don't go!" he cried out and fell to his knees in tears.

"Jack?" a groggy Laurence sauntered into the room, "What's wrong? Did you have a bad dream?"

"Something like that." he rose to his feet, holding onto the cable spool to steady himself.

"Come back to bed, lover. I miss you." Laurence cooed.

"I'll be there in a little while."

"Whatever you were dreaming about shook you up badly. Let me make you feel better."

"In a minute."

Laurence skulked away. Jack sat on the sofa and buried his face in his hands. Why goodbye? What did it mean? Chilled to his bones, he remained on the lumpy sofa. He wished the rock crushing his chest would end his life right then and there. He waited until sunlight crept into the dingy apartment. Then, he fell asleep.

*   *   *

"Code blue, 3 A South, room 302! Code blue, 3 A South, room 302!" the announcement echoed through the deserted waiting room.

*   *   *

"Are you ashamed of me, Jack?" Laurence cast a mournful glance at him across the breakfast table.

"Ashamed? Why? Where's this coming from?"

"Isn't it obvious?"

"I don't understand."

"We've been together for six months now. In all this time, you haven't invited me to stay over at your place once. I don't even know where you live. You haven't introduced me to your friends. We're only together here at my place. We're a couple now, Jack. You should've asked me to move in with you by now. I know you like to take things slow, but this is ridiculous! Don't you love me?"

"Of course I do. Would I be here if I didn't?"

"Some might say you're only here for the sex."

"You know that's not true."

"Then, prove it. Let me move into your place."

Jack shifted in his chair uncomfortably.

"I'm tired of being strung along, Jack. Unless you ask me to move in with you today, this is the end of the road for us."

Jack was painfully silent.

"There's a new guy, isn't there?"
"No. There's no one else, Laurence. Only you."

"I heard you last night before I came into the room. You were calling out a name: Sydney. Who is he?"

"She's my ex-wife."

"A likely story. It's a new boyfriend, isn't it?"

"No. Sydney is my ex-wife."

"Who do you think you're fooling? I've never heard of a woman named Sydney."

"If you don't want to believe me, that's fine, but that is her name: Sydney with two 'y's."

"How do you know? I thought you couldn't remember anything from your past. I thought you couldn't even remember yourself."

"I don't, but I remember her."

"That's just too weird for me, Jack. I'm not buying it. You're playing mind games with me."

"No, I'm not, but I'm too tired to argue with you, Laurence."

"Why were you calling out her name, then?"

"It felt like she was here…in spirit. I felt her presence."

"My mother's friend Lucretia is a medium. Let's go to her and see if she can channel her spirit. If I were you, I'd want proof that she is really dead."

"I don't even want to think about that." Jack rose abruptly, "I have to go."

"So, this is it, then, Jack. We're done."

"Laurence…It doesn't have to be this way."

"I'm not going to be your dirty little secret anymore. I want to be your partner, not your boy toy. I want us to be a proper couple."

"I can't deal with this now, Laurence. What is so wrong with the way things are? We are enjoying each other, sharing special moments. Why can't that be enough?"

"Because I need a commitment. I don't like being trifled with."

"Can we talk about this later?"

"No. I'm tired of getting the run-around. If you love me, you'll commit to me now. Otherwise, we're done. I don't like being used."

"I am not using you."

"Then, why can't I move in with you?"

"Laurence, please. Let's talk about this. I'll bring us some Chinese food tonight. We'll have some wine and talk about things."

"I thought so. If you walk out that door now, don't bother to come back. You and I are over. Goodbye, Jack."

"Laurence..."

"Goodbye, Jack." he pushed him out to the hallway and slammed the door shut behind him.

Jack stumbled down the stairs, tears streaming down his cheeks. The old woman on the main floor was in the hallway again, glaring at him.

Chapter 19/ RAEVYNN

The elderly man on the other side of the Plexiglas divider was oblivious to her. With his downcast eyes, his slumped shoulders, and rumpled hair, he had the air of someone who had resigned himself to the worst fate. She tapped on the divider frantically.

"Excuse me, sir, do you know where we are?"

He did not hear her. They were moving forward effortlessly, at a slight incline, enclosed in a clear pedway elevated above treetops against the night sky. What sort of transportation was this, and how had she arrived here? The vehicle came to a halt and slid open. A clean-shaven young man in a white suit greeted the man and accompanied him to an ornate iron gate. He unlocked the gate for him and locked it again behind him. She stepped down and approached the young man.

"Can you let me in, too?"

"I'm afraid I can't do that." he responded solemnly.

"But you let that man in."

"That was different."

"Is this a private club?"

"I'm afraid I'm not at liberty to divulge any information. You need to return to where you came from."

"I don't know where I am or how I got here. I don't know how to go back. I don't even have a quarter for a phone call...Could I just come in for a short while to use your phone to call someone back home?"

"There are no telephones here, I'm afraid."

"I don't understand."

"Wait here." he disappeared around the corner.

She strained her eyes to see beyond the tall garden wall. Then, a tender embrace transformed her fears to an unexpected calm.

"Brett! It's you! I've missed you so much!" she inhaled her delicate scent.

"Sweetheart, you can't imagine how much I've missed you..." she kissed her hair and pulled her closer.

"Brett, what is this place?...It's heaven, isn't it?"

"In a manner of speaking, sweetheart."

"Is that why that young man wouldn't let me in? Because I'm supposed to go to hell?"

"No, no, no! Sydney, my Sydney, you could never go to hell! He couldn't let you in because you're alive."

"Why can't I just stay here with you?"

"Sweetheart, it's not your time. You need to go back. I'm here to guide you."

"I have nothing to go back to. This is where I want to be."

"Sydney, my love, deep down, a part of you must know you have some more living to do. Everything has to play out as it has been planned."

"I don't feel ready to go back yet, Brett. I want to be with you."

"Sweetheart, they're all worried sick about you back home. When you return, you'll feel ready to face the world. You'll be energized and calm."

"Brett, how do I let you go yet another time?"

"You don't have to. I'm always with you. All you have to do is call my name."

"When am I going to see you again?"

"When it's the right time. No one will be able to tear us apart then. But, now, I have to let you go. You are needed back home."

"I'll miss you."

"I'll miss you, too. I love you, Sydney. Remember, I'm never far."

"I love you, Brett."

Brett faded into the mist as the Plexiglas door slid open for her on her solitary journey home.

* * *

She awoke to the hum of machines keeping her alive in the cold hospital room. Voices could be heard outside her door.

"Only one person at a time, and five minutes each. She's still in critical condition." a nurse was explaining.

"It should be Marin, then." Maxine could be heard, "They came all the way from John's Bay to see her."

"Five minutes." the nurse reminded them.

The door opened softly. Footsteps approached her bed.

"Sydney, it's me, Marin." the shaky voice spoke, "I've been so worried about you...Please come back to us...You've always been my rock; now, I want to be yours. I'll do anything to have you back...You're my family. You're the only family Brette, Sam and I have now. We love you. Please come back to us..."

Marin was in tears now, and Sydney felt powerless for not being able to comfort her. She attempted to move her fingers, but her body refused to obey her. Marin wept inconsolably at her feet until the nurse entered the room.

"Your five minutes are up."

"Get better, Sydney. I love you." Marin called out as she was being escorted out.

"Can my daughter see her next?" Marin could be heard from the hallway.

"How old is she?"

"Twelve."

"Well, seeing as you folks are from out of town...Maybe for two minutes. It has to be very short."

"Thank you."

"Grandma Sydney..." a tiny voice murmured, "I miss you...Please get better soon...I made you a card. I'm going to put it beside you on the nightstand.

When you're able to open your eyes, you'll see it…I love you, Grandma Sydney…" she sat on the chair weeping.

"Time to leave now, dear." the nurse entered the room to lead her back to the waiting area. "Only one more visitor for today." she stated matter-of-factly.

"Maybe Daniel should be the one." Olga was saying, "He's a therapist, so he'd know exactly what to say to make her want to come back."

"Yes, go ahead, Dan." Eli agreed.

Daniel entered her room and sat on the chair by the window.

"I think they're giving me too much credit, pretty lady. I don't think I can be calm and collected enough to say the right things. I'm just grateful that you're hanging in there, fighting like a trooper to come back to us."

He sat with her in silence until the nurse came in to remind him his five minutes were up.

* * *

She glanced up from her book when she heard the tentative knock. Through the narrow glass in the door, she could discern a diminutive female form with a mass of long black curls, black-rimmed glasses and a long, loose, black garment.

"Come in." she called out.

"Sydney Goldstein?" the young woman stepped inside, "Well, of course you are. I mean, I wanted to meet you."

"Meet me?" she eyed her quizzically.

"I'm Raevynn Morningstar." she reached out to shake her hand, "I'm the one who called for help."

"You're the one who saved my life!" she squeezed her hand, "Thank you! I'm very grateful to you."

"I just happened to be walking home when I saw two boys running out of your store. I went right over and saw you lying on the floor. I yelled out at people on the street to call the police while I stayed with you. I didn't want to touch anything, not even the phone, so the cops could dust for fingerprints in the store."

"Thank you. I'm very grateful."

"I had no idea who you were at the time, but I later found out you are the woman who took Warren Horncastle to court. You're my idol."

"It's all water under the bridge now."

"What you did was amazing. You're a trailblazer for all women who've been victims of violence at the hands of their partners."

"You're very kind. All of that was a lifetime ago."

"I wasn't living here at that time, but I've heard so much about you from the women I work with."

"All of that business was a very long time ago. The circumstances have changed drastically since then."

"I've heard, later you've had one husband go missing, lost another husband to suicide, and a female lover who died of cancer…Wow…I don't know how you survived. You must be such a strong woman."

"Far from it."

"Don't be so modest. I can't think of too many women who could go through all of that and still be standing."

Sydney smiled uncomfortably at the irony of having this dubious honor bestowed upon her. Raevynn's small dark eyes were darting back and forth, taking in every detail of Sydney's appearance.

"I see so much of myself in you." the younger woman continued, "I was a battered wife myself. I ended up homeless and addicted to alcohol and drugs. Thankfully, my aunt and uncle took me in and I started attending AA meetings. I've been clean and sober now for eight years. I finished my Social Work degree and worked for three years before I decided to forge my own path a couple of years ago. Now, I work with marginalized and abused women."

"That's very impressive, Raevynn. I'm so glad you overcame the adversity and you are using your experiences to help other women. I truly admire you for that."

"Thank you. I've faced so much oppression from so many people in this town."

"I'm so sorry. People in Beavertown can be such right-wing rednecks."

"I'm like a cat. I always land on my feet. I can't work within the system anymore. I've ruffled too many feathers."

"I can certainly relate to that."

"Even agencies that are there to help women are really quite misogynistic."

"No doubt."

"Women who have been abused come to me for counselling. I have broken free from the shackles of male domination. I am free, powerful and in charge of my own destiny. No one can keep me down."

"That's remarkable."

"Ms. Goldstein..."

"Please call me Sydney."

"Is it all right if I use your bathroom?"

"Of course."

Sydney returned to her book, a collection of Shirley Jackson's short stories when a familiar voice remarked sarcastically:

"Well, well, well. If it isn't the perpetual victim."

"Celia." she rolled her eyes.

"Ms. 'Woe Is Me'. You'll do anything to get attention."

"Yes. I hired a couple of goons to rob my business, and beat me to a pulp, just for the hell of it. What do you want, Celia?"

"I heard about what happened and wanted to see the damage for myself."

"Now that you've seen it, are you happy? Does it satisfy your sadistic urges?"

"I can see all these years in high society haven't improved your manners. You can take the girl out of the ghetto but you can't take the ghetto out of the girl."

"Speak for yourself, Celia."

"No wonder none of your relationships last. Jack abandoned you. Tony couldn't stomach being married to you, so he chose death over a life with you. And, Brett only stayed with you because she was dying. She wouldn't have given you the time of day, had she been healthy. You can't hang on to anyone, can you, Sydney? They all eventually leave you. You really are a sick woman. You ought to be put away, so you can't lure yet another unsuspecting victim into your web."

"Ooo. Beware the kiss of the scorpion woman." Sydney smirked.

"You destroy people's lives. Look at Warren now: A cripple. A vital, exciting man like that, cut down in his prime."

"What are you even talking about, Celia? You don't even make sense."

"Playing dumb, I see."

"I have no idea what you're talking about. What happened to him?"

"It was in all the papers, and on television."

"I was not in any condition to be reading newspapers or watching T.V."

"If you don't know, I am not going to tell you just to make you gloat."

They heard the flushing of the toilet, the sound of the faucet, and Raevynn emerged from the bathroom.

"Get out!" Raevynn stood before Celia, pointing her index finger menacingly at her, "Get out now! You're disturbing Sydney! I'll call security and have you escorted out if you don't get out right now!"

"Who do you think you are?"

"I'm Sydney's friend."

"My time is too valuable to be wasting with the likes of you, anyway." Celia threw her head back, "I suggest you get some therapy with one of my colleagues, Sydney. You need it."

"Elitist bitch!" Raevynn screamed.

"What's all the commotion in here? I could hear you ladies all the way from the nurses' station." a nurse burst in.

"This woman's been harassing Sydney. I've been trying to get rid of her." Raevynn informed her.

"You need to leave now. Both of you." the nurse stated sternly.

"Please, let Raevynn stay." Sydney pleaded, "She was helping me. I don't know what I would've done if she hadn't been here."

"All right, then." the nurse motioned Celia toward the hallway, "You'll have to leave, Ma'am."

"Thank you, Raevynn." Sydney said, "I really appreciate that."

"I couldn't believe that psycho bitch! Are you all right?" Raevynn sat at the edge of the bed and massaged her arm, "You've been through a horrible ordeal. Seeing her was the last thing you needed."

"I'm all right, really."

"You are an incredible woman, Sydney. I feel honored to be in your presence."

"You're very kind."

"I think we should keep in touch. Maybe we could have coffee once you're back on your feet."

"That would be very nice."

"I'll let you get some rest now."

"I doubt I'll be getting any rest now, after hearing about Warren being hurt. Now, it makes sense why my cousin Dottie wasn't around earlier. They were telling me she was on holiday, but, knowing her, it didn't make sense."

"From what I've heard, he was in a skiing accident in Colorado and your cousin went there to stay with him until he was ready to be moved to the local hospital. I hope that helps."

"Thank you. It does."

"It's so cool that you and he have ended up being friends. It's a testament to what a beautiful person you are."

"You're very kind, Raevynn."

"I'll get going now." she rose, "Are you glad I came?"

"Very glad."

"I'll be back to visit you again. I'll visit you at the music store, too, when you are back at work.

Maybe we'll have lunch at one of the new delis they've opened downtown."

"Sounds lovely."

"Take care, Sydney."

"You, too, Raevynn."

Raevynn waved on her way out and closed the door behind her.

Chapter 20/ SEA GREEN GODDESS

"What's the deal with you and the crow chick? Is there something going on there?"

"Nothing's going on, Warren." Sydney smiled, putting the brakes on his wheelchair and rearranging his scarf around his neck, "Why don't we stop here for a while and take in the view?"

"No problem." he buttoned his cabled cardigan, "It's nearly May, but you'd never know it."

She stroked his white mane and sat on the bench beside him, winding her long scarf tighter around her neck.

"I think she's taking advantage of you." he said, not taking his eyes off the young couples in athletic gear walking their dogs by the water, "She seems to be taking up so much of your time, asking you for favors."

"She did save my life, Warren."

"That does not entitle her to abuse your generosity. Those posters she hung up in your store window could really hurt your business. She's advertising her workshops and what-not, furthering her own agenda, but all that New Age and Radical Feminism stuff isn't exactly compatible with your vintage music shop. I'd be careful, if I were you."

"I'm just trying to be helpful."

"You're too helpful, if you ask me. People are going to think you believe in that stuff."

"I know you're right. I just feel everyone needs someone who believes in them."

"If she's telling you no one else understands her or supports her, better watch out. Those are red flags. I know chicks. I can smell a scam a mile away."

"You know, Marin, Eli and Daniel don't like her, either."

"There you go. It's not just me. You're too kind-hearted to your own detriment."

"She's had a hard life."

"Haven't we all?"

She reached out to pat his hand.

"There's something unsettling about her. I can't put my finger on it, but something about her disturbs me."

"Marin said she's noticed me feeling down and stressed out since meeting Raevynn. I've also been getting headaches lately. I thought it might be the after effect of my injuries, but my doctor said I've recovered fully and no such things should be happening. Marin thinks it might be some sort of a spell Rae has concocted."

"Wouldn't put it past her. She's into Wicca and all sorts of those dark arts, isn't she?"

"She says it's all part of New Age."

"She's gaslighting you. I know all about con games. I've been guilty of indulging in them with chicks. I recognize the signs." he winked at her.

She patted his arm.

"Daniel warned me about the love-bombing." she said.

"People like the crow are uncanny in their ability to detect vulnerability in their potential victims. You're a prime target, Stormy."

"Thanks a lot." she laughed.

"Your beautiful soul shines through those big wounded eyes of yours. Cads like me salivate around chicks like you."

"You're so good for my ego, Warren."

"Now that I've mended my ways, I can help you recognize all the warning signs."

"I appreciate that."

"You have no defenses, Stormy. People take advantage of you so easily. Granted, it's not just cads who find you irresistible. Nice guys fall in love with your soft, nurturing ways. You need to nurture and protect yourself, too, or everyone's going to keep walking all over you."

She stood, leaned down and kissed his cheek.

"How's Marin, anyway? She hasn't been around for a long time."

"Her MS is getting worse. She's not able to go on long car rides, but we keep in touch through phone calls and letters."

"Only an hour and a half away, but you have to write and phone."

"That hour and a half is torture for her."

"It's very sad."

"Life is sad." she sat down on the bench again, "Sadness outweighs the joy. We live purely for the hope of finding joy around the next corner."

"Only to be disillusioned yet again."

"Those rare moments of extreme joy we actually find are always taken away from us so quickly."

"Were you disappointed when you came back from your near death experience?"

"Very. I wanted to stay on the other side to see my parents again, but I wasn't permitted to stay any longer."

"At least, you got to see Brett. What about Tony?"

"No. I didn't see him, but he's visited me in dreams to let me know he's been in agreement with the choices I've made since I lost him and that he's with Adele now for eternity."

"That makes sense. Adele was the love of his life. No offense."

"None taken. I'm very happy for him."

"Me, too. You're a safe harbor for all broken lost souls, Stormy. You don't even realize the impact you have on people."

"I appreciate that more than you know, Warren. I treasure your friendship."

"Let's get out of here before we get too soppy and become fodder for more gossip."

"It's getting too chilly, anyway." she released the brakes of his wheelchair.

"Fred's going to send out a search party if we're not back soon."

They laughed.

"Fred's been a reliable caregiver for you. I'm glad you found someone like him. Dottie did a fantastic job of getting a dependable contractor on short notice to make the guest house wheelchair-accessible again. It's very comfortable and modern."

"Are you coming back tomorrow, Stormy?"

"Of course." she led him across Waterloo Row, "Fred must have your supper ready."

"He's quite a good cook. I've been putting on weight lately."

"I didn't notice it." she led him up the ramp to his front door.

Before she had the chance to ring the doorbell, Fred opened the door. The aroma of his beef stew wafted out to the entry.

"It smells good." she remarked.

"Stay for supper." Warren said.

"Yes. Please stay, Ma'am." Fred insisted, "I made enough for a crowd."

"Well…"

"Please."

"All right, then. I'll stay. But on one condition: I'll do the clean-up." she closed the door behind her.

* * *

They followed the stern middle-aged couple out of the elevator to the whisper-rose marble hallway. The woman turned around and glanced in their direction with a crooked smile. Her flowing dress in magenta silk shimmered under the enormous rosette-shaped crystal chandeliers. Despite its simple cut, the expertly tailored garment draped subtly, emphasizing her curves. Her scowling companion with the bulbous nose was tapping his feet impatiently. The woman's heavily made-up dark eyes were focused on Jack. She sized him up with a bemused smirk before slipping an arm through her companion's. Once they were out of earshot, Aydin snickered.

"You've still got it, you silver fox, you."

A beet-red Jack shook his head.

"Aren't you glad you came with us?" Aydin led the way to the lounge.

"I feel like I've been here before." Jack said, "There's something so familiar about this place."

"I wouldn't be surprised if you were here during your touring years." Kent said, "Maybe you'll get your memory back, being here again."

"I wish, but I doubt it."

"Just soak in the beauty of the city and enjoy yourself." Kent said, leading them to a table with an unobstructed view of the stage.

The darkened lounge was resplendent in festive purple – from the walls, to the floor, ceiling, lights, tables and chairs. A blond young man was concluding his set with "Stranger In Paradise".

"That's you." Aydin remarked, "You're a stranger in paradise."

"That's how I feel. This city is definitely paradise."

"Istanbul is the most beautiful city in the world."

"I have no doubt about that. If I were fortunate enough to be born here, I would never leave. I'm sorry if that sounded judgmental. I didn't mean to imply…"

"No worries, Jack. No offence taken." Kent reassured him, "Aydin and I would've done the same, but our parents had other plans for us at the time."

"I'm sorry."

"A foreign education is considered prestigious here, though our universities are every bit as good, even superior. Our parents believed New York was the best place to live, in the entire world." Kent smiled sardonically.

"We grew up in Bebek, which is a district very close to here. Neither one of us had such lofty ideals. Our parents consider us the black sheep of our families."

"For being gay?"

"Not so much. Mainly for not pursuing postgraduate studies. Our sisters are all doctors and engineers, so they are the golden children."

"So, you two grew up together, your families knew each other and you both went through a major move across the world as kids. But, in the end, you're together and pursuing your own dreams."

"We might be living our dreams, but being cut off from your birth place is like a wound that never heals. You survive, you adjust, but you never heal. Even regular visits don't soothe the ache, because once you've been transplanted, you never quite fit in back home again either, so, we're strangers in paradise right along with you, Jack."

"I'm very sorry, guys. I wish all three of us could retire early and move here."

"Ah, if only that could be possible." Aydin sighed.

A uniformed waiter approached their table with a wide grin.

"Aydin *Abi!* Kent *Abi! Hos Geldiniz!*"

Embraces were exchanged.

"Eren, meet our friend, Jack." Kent said.

"*Hos Geldiniz*, Jack *Bey.*" the young man shook his hand, enunciating carefully, "I hope you enjoy your stay."

"Thank you." Jack smiled conventionally.

"What would you like?"

"Two bottles of *raki,* please, Eren." Kent said, "And some *meze.*"

"Coming right up. It sure is nice to see you."

"What's *raki*?" Jack whispered.

"It's a Turkish speciality. You can't come to Turkey and not try *raki.*"

"What's mez...mez...?"

"*Meze* is a cold snack served with alcohol. Mainly nuts."

"How do you pronounce it?"

"Pretend it's a French word: Mezee."

"What is Hosh-Gal-Dennis? They said it at the front desk, too."

"It means welcome."

"What is *Abi*?"

"Brother. Friends call each other brother or sister."

"You two are *abis* and I'm a bay, whatever that means."

"*Bey* is sir."

"This is going to be a very interesting night." Jack leaned back.

The young singer was taking his bows and leaving the stage.

"Mert is very popular with the ladies." Aydin said, "You just wait till you see the next set." he smirked.

"Surtuk Sureyya." Kent groaned.

"What was that again?" Jack asked.

"*Surtuk* means 'one who gets around', and Sureyya is her given name. Everyone calls her Surtuk Sureyya because of her reputation." Aydin winked, "She's quite a looker, too."

"Sounds intriguing. You weren't exaggerating when you told me Turkish women were exceptionally beautiful and scantily clad."

Their *raki* and *meze* were served. Aydin filled each glass half with *raki* and half with the spring water served in individual bottles. Jack watched in amazement as the clear liquid turned milky. He took a sip and immediately put it back down.

"It must be an acquired taste." he said, "What's in it?"

"Aniseed."

"Tastes like licorice. What is aniseed?"

"It's used as a spice and a flavoring in a variety of Turkish foods." Kent explained.

"It's different. I feel like I'm drinking liquid licorice."

"I'm going to make sure I remember that." Aydin laughed, "Liquid licorice!"

They heard a drumroll. Amid shouts, applause and whistles, a slender figure in a sea green sequined low-cut gown with thigh-high slits on each side was slithering up to the stage, blowing kisses at the audience. Jack froze as she broke into strains of Barry Manilow's "Ready To Take A Chance Again". He gulped down his glass of *raki*. Aydin poured him another, which he also drank swiftly. Kent and Aydin's voices were becoming a distant hum. He was the only one there and she was singing just for him. The sea green goddess slithered through the maze of tables and stood beside him, one hand on his shoulder. Taking his hand in hers, she led him back to the stage with her. His feet felt detached from his body as he followed her. His surroundings were fading in and out of view. The lights were blinding him. The band sounded discordant. Looking at her close-up under the bright lights, he realized Sureyya appeared older than he had initially believed, albeit more alluring and intoxicating than any woman of any age he had been fortunate enough to meet. As the song came to an end, she took the microphone in both hands and spoke in impeccable English:

"Ladies and Gentlemen. We have a very special guest with us today. The international singing sensation Jack Chandler is here. He and I are going to sing a duet for you."

"We are?" he whispered quizzically.

"'Fly Me To The Moon'. Hit it, Murat!" she motioned to someone in the band behind them and took his hand again; he hung on for dear life, as he felt his footing slipping away.

Having survived the impromptu duet, he attempted to leave the stage amid shouts of "Encore" from the audience, however, she pulled him back.

"I feel sick." he whispered to Sureyya.

The band members behind him broke into laughter. Sureyya turned around swiftly to admonish them in Turkish. He detected the word "sick".

"What did they find so funny?" he asked her.

"In Turkish, 'sick' means something very different."

"What does it mean?"

"Something you and I are going to be doing later tonight." she winked.

He was speechless. She laughed in amusement, watching him turn red.

"One more song? After that, we can both leave. I'll ask Filiz, the backup singer to finish my set tonight."

"Okay. One more song."

"Let's do 'How Do You Keep The Music Playing?'"

At the end of the song, once again, the audience was shouting "Encore". Sureyya took the microphone again.

"Ladies and gentlemen. I'm afraid our guest is not feeling well tonight. Jetlag, you know. My colleague Filiz Moray is going to be entertaining you the rest of the evening. Thank you and good night. *Iyi geceler.*" she blew kisses.

"*Iyi geceler.*" he waved self-consciously, grateful that he had learned how to say "good night" in Turkish.

Screams from the audience followed as she led him away through the back of the stage.

"How did you know who I was?"

"You have a lot of die-hard fans in Istanbul, Jack." she caressed his cheek, leading him into her dressing room and shutting the door behind them, "I still remember the time you were here in '76, right here at this hotel. I was married then, so I didn't have the chance to get to know you. You haven't aged at all in two decades. Handsome as ever. The hotel's been buzzing all day with news that Jack Chandler's in the building. I spotted you the moment I locked eyes with you."

"You're very kind."

"You're a very nice guy. It's refreshing to see that. Grand Tarabya Hotel hosts many concerts by big international stars in the reception hall. None of them are nice like you."

"Thank you."

"Would you mind unzipping me, Jack?" she turned her back.

His trembling hands fumbled with the long, delicate zipper. She let her gown fall to her feet, and emerged from it with a black push-up bra and black bikini panties. He gathered up her gown and handed it to her, avoiding eye contact.

"*Merci.*" she said, kicking off her high heels, placing her sea green gown on a satin hanger and hanging it from a hook.

She removed a red crop top from a hanger and pulled it down over her head. The denim mini skirt on the chair completed her ensemble. She stepped into a pair of red platform sandals. Slinging a slender white bag across her chest, she opened the door.

"Let's go." she took his arm.

"Where are we going?" he asked sheepishly.

"My apartment." she laughed.

Sureyya led him through a labyrinth of narrow, winding cobblestone streets, past Victorian-era houses with second-storey bay windows, to a block of stucco Art Deco apartment buildings in pink, white, and coral nestled in lush gardens. She opened the elaborate iron gate of a pink building. The flagstone courtyard was filled with cats huddled by the entrance. Sureyya bent down to pat each one and spoke softly to them in Turkish. He noticed multiple dishes of cat food by the flowerbeds.

"Are all of them yours?" he asked.

"None of them are." she laughed, "They're neighborhood cats. They belong to no one. They're free spirits. We all leave dishes of cat food and milk outside the building. I'm quite partial to my princess here, though." she picked up a white fluffy cat and kissed the top of her head, "Pamuk is my baby."

Jack patted her tentatively.

"Come on up." she put Pamuk down and opened the door to the building with her key.

He followed her up the pink terrazzo stairs to a pink door on the second floor. Another key unlocked it.

"Make yourself at home." she removed her shoes and put on a pair of burgundy sequined velvet slippers, "But please remove your shoes first."

"Okay." he obeyed and put on the navy blue men's slippers she provided.

"*Hos Geldin.*" she said, "Would you like a drink?"

"I think I've had enough to drink tonight."

"Your friends got you to try *raki*, didn't they?" she laughed.

"That stuff is strong."

"I'm not a big fan. I prefer sweeter drinks. Why don't you have a little something with me? I have Cinzano, and rose liqueur."

"Rose liqueur? I've never heard of it."

"It's a Turkish specialty. Made with real rose petals." she produced an ornate bottle and a liqueur glass from a kitchen cupboard and poured herself a miniature drink, "Want some?"

"Maybe I'd better wait for another time."

"When you don't feel so sick?" she winked, "Will you excuse me?" she walked down a dark corridor.

Jack glanced around the apartment. White lace curtains, white leather sectional sofas, glass and metal tables, a pale pink area rug, shell pink walls, crystal chandeliers...all things light and airy and feminine...He wondered how she was able to afford an apartment like this on a lounge singer's salary. Perhaps, she had a benefactor. Obviously an open relationship, whether mutually agreed upon or not.

Sureyya returned, her blonde curls now loose and falling past her shoulders. She was dressed in an almond pink lace peignoir and marabou slippers. His heart skipped a beat. He surrendered to her rose-flavored kisses. Her fingers skillfully removed his tie and shirt. She planted tender kisses on his chest and led him to the bedroom. Her flimsy peignoir fell to the floor. Her flawless skin was pure white, even in the dim light from the hallway. He noticed in amazement that she had no pubic hair. Then, her octopus tentacles wound around him and she swallowed him up in the dark, carrying him to a dimension from which there was no return.

* * *

He awakened to the musical call of street vendors advertising their wares. Surprisingly, he was not hung over. Just refreshed and alive. Then, he realized Sureyya was not beside him. He jumped out of bed in panic and tripped over his clothes on the floor.

"Good morning, Jack!" he heard her voice down the hall.

"Good morning. Where are you?" he called out.

"I'll be with you soon. Help yourself to breakfast."

He walked toward the kitchen. Through the open bathroom door, he saw her on the toilet. She waved. He waved back, and followed her instructions. He pulled up a barstool to the kitchen island where an omelette-like creation was on a plate. On one side was a glass of orange juice and on the other side was an hourglass-shaped glass filled with a reddish brown liquid which he assumed to be tea.

"Dig in." she was now behind him.

"Aren't you having some, too?"

"I already ate. I had some toast and cheese. This *menemen* is just for you."

"*Menemen*?"

"Um hum. It's scrambled eggs with ground beef, tomatoes and peppers."

"*Menemen*. Very manly name." he laughed.

"I didn't know how many sugars you take in your tea."

"I just take it plain. What a pretty color it is in that clear glass."

"In Turkey, we drink it out of special tea glasses, so we can be sure it's the right color. It has to be reddish. We call that rabbit's blood. No one puts milk in their tea. It has to be a clear liquid. It's steeped a special way."

He noticed a ceramic tea kettle with pink roses on her stovetop with a teapot in a matching print nesting on top of it.

"I'm going to introduce you to so many Turkish delicacies."

"If last night is any indication of things to come, I'm all in." he simpered.

"You've only dipped your toes so far. Hurry up and finish your breakfast. I have made plans for us for today."

"What are they?"

"It's a surprise."

"Can you give me a hint?"

"No. You'll just have to wait and see. But, first, I have other plans for us." she rubbed his neck.

He wondered what he had ever done to deserve so much pleasure, to meet a woman like Sureyya beyond his wildest imaginings. As they lay in the afterglow, she became aware of his eyes on her hairless bits.

"It's the custom here to shave down there."

"Sorry if I was staring."

"It's okay. Women in America don't shave down there, I know." she patted his stomach, "Do you have a special lady waiting for you back home?"

"No."

"That's good. I'm sure you break a lot of hearts."

"Not intentionally."

"Not intentionally! You're adorable! Why don't we get tattoos of each other's names?"

"Each other's names? What about just initials?"

"Just initials? That's no fun."

"It might be...more affordable."

"Don't worry about cost. I know a guy. I can get us a discount. I would like to see my name on your chest."

"Can't we just do initials?"

"Why? Are you ashamed of me?"

"Of course not. You're my Sea Green Goddess, Sureyya."

"Then, why don't you want my name on your chest? Don't you like my name?"

"I think it's the most beautiful name I've ever heard. I just don't like pain. Tattoos probably hurt a lot. If it's just initials, the pain will be over with faster."

"Tattoos don't hurt at all. The rose on my back and the cat on my ankle didn't hurt one bit. But, fine. We'll do it your way. Just initials."

"Thank you."

"Come on. We'd better get going. We can shower together, to save water."

He was perfectly content to let her lead the way and make the decisions. If this was a drunken dream, he was not prepared to awaken just yet.

As they stepped outside, he noticed an elderly man in a plaid shirt and department store jeans and sneakers was patting a gray tabby in the courtyard. He greeted Sureyya in Turkish. She greeted him back and introduced him to the man in Turkish.

"*Merhaba.*" the man with the kind blue eyes smiled.

"*Merhaba.*" he responded awkwardly.

The man said something else in Turkish and more pleasantries were exchanged between them. Sureyya concluded the conversation with a wave. She turned to Jack and translated.

"He hopes you'll enjoy your stay in our city." she took his arm.

"Very nice man."

"Yes. Uncle Halit is a sweet, fatherly man. He adores that cat. He calls Tekir his son."

"What is cat in Turkish?"

"*Kedi.*"

"*Kedi*. I like that." he smiled, "What was the name of the *kedi* you liked?"

"Pamuk."

"Pamuk. That's too hard to remember. I'll just call her Pam. Pam the *kedi*."

Chapter 21/ AS THE CROW FLIES

She heard the jingle of the door being opened by a customer and turned around to find herself face to face with those wild eyebrows.

"I want to talk to you." the balding man stated matter-of-factly, "You may not know who I am…"

"I know exactly who you are." she said coldly.

"Good. I'll cut to the chase, then. I want you to stay away from my daughter and granddaughter."

"They're not your daughter and granddaughter." she glared at him, "Brett Morrow was their late mother and grandmother."

"I don't want them around the likes of you."

"That is not your decision to make."

"If you do not keep your distance from Leigh and Nora, I'll get a restraining order against you."

"Their names are Marin and Brettiella."

"Not anymore. We call the shots now. And you are not welcome in their lives anymore."

"I'd prefer to hear it from Marin herself."

"You're an unwholesome influence on them. It upsets my wife that they are still consorting with the likes of you. I have to protect my family."

"So, Marin and Brette don't get a say in this."

"They want us to be in their lives now. They feel no more connection to you. It's up to me and my wife to protect and guide them."

"They should be taking out a restraining order against the two of you!"

"They've made their choice. They want a traditional family with parents and grandparents. You've been warned: Keep your distance. Don't try to contact them in any way." the short man with the rounded shoulders stormed out with a loud jingle.

She locked the door and changed the sign to "Closed". The rock in her chest refused to dissolve into tears. It sat there, immovable and permanent.

* * *

She opened the door to find Raevynn smiling broadly.

"I happened to be in the neighborhood, and I thought I'd drop in to see if you're home."

"Come in. It's good to see you, Rae." she stood aside to let her in.

"I love your house. You're lucky to have such a swanky place, Sydney." Raevynn scrutinized her surroundings.

"It's kind of messy right now."

"You've got packing boxes. Are you moving?"

"No. Just cleaning out some old stuff."

"Are you getting rid of your knickknacks? Can I have a peek?"

"Nothing like that. Just some old pictures. I'm going to store them in the attic."

"So, you don't want them anymore?"

"Some day, someone might want them. But I have no use for them."

"Sounds intriguing. Old lovers?"

"Hardly. Let's just forget about it. I'm glad to see you."

"Me, too." Raevynn embraced her.

"Tell me how you've been. I'll put on some jasmine tea. I know it's your fave."

"I went by the store this morning and it was closed. I thought you had Saturday morning hours."

"We normally do, but something unexpected came up."

"Want to talk about it?"

"No, it's not important. Tell me how you're doing."

"I'm doing great. Never better. You've been such an inspiration to me, Sydney."

"Me? That's nice to hear."

"After meeting you, I did a lot of soul-searching. I've come out as a lesbian in a big way now. It's been so liberating to be surrounded by friends and lovers at my collective. Those women are so nurturing and accepting."

"I'm happy for you."

"Sydney, I get the feeling you're surrounded by negative energy."

"You're telling me." she rolled her eyes.

"Energy vampires are taking advantage of your big heart and dragging you down. You need to cut all ties with the people in your life and forge a new path for yourself."

"I don't know anything anymore, Rae."

"You are a beautiful woman, Sydney. You have beauty, brains, talent. But you have a heavy heart. I'm sure Brett would want you to be healed, so you could move on with your life."

"I'll be all right."

"I can heal you. I assure you, I'm very good. I could open up a whole new world for you. Come on, let's go for a walk in the park. Fresh air will do you good."

"That's a good idea."

"Forget about the tea. Let's just enjoy the day."

The scent of the primrose bushes in the park was intoxicating. Captivated by the furious pilgrimage of the bees Sydney was unaware of Raevynn beside her.

"You and Brett were singers, were you not?" Raevynn attempted to divert her attention.

"Yes."

"I'm a singer, too. I would like to sing for you. I reserve my voice only for very special people. I could probably make a lot of money singing, too, but God gave me this talent, so I could heal people. I want to heal you, Sydney." Raevynn broke into a New Age song with no discernable melody and lyrics that feigned profound spirituality.

Sydney's gaze was fixed on the distant clearing in the thickly wooded section of the park, visible through the intricate lacework of branches, where a raven was feasting on a wounded robin. A cold chill went through her, even in the sweltering Beavertown heat.

* * *

In the sundrenched living room, she settled into a corner of the sofa and encircled her hands around the steaming mug of coffee. Mornings in this room with Brett danced through her mind...Brett pulling her to her feet to dance, the two of them tumbling down like wooden building blocks...their laughter turning to tears...Moments like those, she relived each day with searing pain. From the enlarged print of the photo she had taken on the deserted beach in Maine, Brett was smiling at her. She wanted to bury herself under a fragrant duvet cover and weep...weep until all life abandoned her body.

She had made a promise to Brett to take care of Marin and Brettiella. Her heart was being ripped out of her chest yet again. She would not allow Henry and Emerald to snatch her loved ones away from her. She ran up the two flights of stairs to the attic and opened the boxes one by one. She kissed the photographs and held them to her chest.

"As long as I'm living and breathing, you'll always have my unconditional love and support. I love all of you very much. I'll never abandon you." she remembered telling Marin.

"No one's going to force me to break my promise." she spoke out loud, "I'm not going to let Henry and Emerald intimidate me."

She wiped her tears with her fingers and returned downstairs. It was too lovely a day to spend indoors. She slipped out the back door. Eli was laboring away at his tiny patch of a vegetable garden in front of the guest house.

"Sydney! You're out early!" he rose to greet her.

"It's such a nice day. I wanted to take advantage of it. Would you mind some company?"

"I'd love it." he removed his gardening gloves and placed them on a large rock before embracing her.

"You look like you could use a cold drink, Eli. Would you like some ice tea?"

"That would be lovely."

"I'll be right back." she patted his shoulder.

Her life was unfolding in peace, tranquility, and friendship. She had all she needed and could ever want.

*　*　*

Raevynn was standing on the porch in a long black dress with elaborate embroidery, her long, wild hair falling around her face in total disarray.

"I've been thinking an awful lot about you lately, Sydney." she hugged her, "You were pretty upset about something the last time I saw you."

"It's okay now."

"That's good. Who are you listening to?" she turned around, "It sounds so lovely."

"It's Eydie Gorme: 'It Never Entered My Mind'."

"What a voice! You have such good taste in music. The last time I was here, you were playing Helen Reddy."

"'Peaceful ' on repeat. She kept me from smashing things."

"I love Helen Reddy, too."

"A gentle, unassuming soul."

"Like you, Sydney."

"I don't know about that, Rae."

"I've never known anyone as nurturing and generous as you, Sydney. Do you know what a beautiful person you are?" Raevynn's arms enclosed her unexpectedly, "I never want us to part. Sydney, you have the most perfect soul. I want us to be friends for life." she caressed her hair and back.

Sydney's tears broke free. She wept inconsolably in Raevynn's arms as Raevynn rocked her and sang softly. She led Sydney to the sofa and guided her head to her own shoulder.

* * *

She opened the door with her key and stepped tentatively into the hall. He emerged from the back of the house, wheeling himself with remarkable skill.

"Hi there." she smiled.

"Hi yourself." he flashed his dimples.

"I just saw your physiotherapist driving off. How did today's session go?"

"As well as can be expected."

"It's coming along; just be patient. Why don't we have a stroll along The Green?"

"Yes, Ma'am. You love bossing me around, don't you?"

"I'm going to treat you to lunch, too, at 'Ruthie's Restaurant'."

"Next, you'll have me ballroom dancing."

"You never know."

She led him down the driveway to the sidewalk.

"Why are you spending so much time with me, Stormy?"

"Why would you ask me that? Do you want me to go away?" she paused.

"Surely, you must have better things to do than babysit a cripple."

"Warren, please don't do this. I look forward to our daily visits, strolls, dinners, long talks. This is where I want to be."

"I don't want your pity, Stormy."

"It's not pity. I'm here because I want to be with you, because I enjoy our time together."

"You've got a store and a club to run. How do you find the time?"

"Greeney's the one who runs the store and Peggy's the brains behind the club. So, you can't get rid of me that easily."

"I thought Rowena was taking up all your free time."

"Rowena? Who's that?"

"Rowena Messer. Your crow chick's real name. She might call herself Raevynn Morningstar, but she's just plain old Rowena Messer from some farming community in Nova Scotia. She's lived in Vancouver for the past twenty some years in hippie communes. Has a rap sheet, too – mainly for possession and petty theft."

"You've always believed she had ulterior motives. I should've listened to you."

"She's been laying it on so thick with you, I knew she was up to something. I didn't trust her from the start."

"Thank you for looking out for me." she stepped in front of him, kissed his cheek, and clasped his hand.

"Who'd ever have thought you and I would be thick as thieves?" he laughed softly.

"We've been friends for a long time."

"With me hitting on you every chance I had and you rebuffing me every time. It took my becoming disabled to bring us closer together on a deep level."

"We've always had an inexplicable connection, Warren."

"A Scorpio connection."

"We've always had each other's backs."

"Not always. You seem to have a short memory."

"We resolved our differences. When the chips were down, you were there for me in a big way."

"If you only knew everything that went down at that time."

"Do you think you'll ever fill in the blanks for me?"

"Perhaps, some day."

"Now, I want to be here for you, Warren. You are very special to me."

"You're playing with fire, Stormy. I'm a selfish bastard. When you fall in love with someone, I'll do everything in my power to fuck it up for you. I'm not capable of being altruistic. I don't want you to be happy; I want you all to myself."

"This is where I want to be." she reached over his shoulder and squeezed his hand. He was grateful she could not see his tears.

* * *

"I've been calling you for days, but you've been incommunicado!" Raevynn burst in, "Are you trying to avoid me, Sydney?"

"No, Raevynn. I haven't been around much lately. I was needed at work for inventory and other things. I had a lot going on."

"Like spending time with Warren? My friend Zilla saw you two together at Ruthie's Restaurant. Are you thinking about getting involved with him again?"

"We're old friends."

"I don't know how you can be friends with him after what he did to you!"

"We've both evolved since then."

"You can't get involved with him again! The moment your guard is down, he'll do the same thing. Leopards don't change their spots. It would be a disaster."

"Warren and I have a friendship that we both appreciate."

"You're being totally selfish! You just want to get your needs met by sleeping with the nearest available person."

"What? Sleeping with him? Raevynn, we're old pals; we get each other. We're not sleeping together."

"You have to get away from him! Believe me, I know what is best for you. I was sent by God to heal you. That takes time. You can't focus your energy elsewhere. Other people will prevent you from getting close to God. You need to stand back and take stock of all your relationships. All of them are dysfunctional. Warren is a narcissist who abused you and raped you."

"He's done a lot for me as a friend since then. He's had my back when I was at my worst."

"Look at your history: There was Jack Chandler: A weak Mama's Boy who proved to be totally unreliable. And, Tony Horncastle, an emotional wreck..."

"Those relationships were beautiful. Besides, all of us are flawed."

"Then, there was Brett...Yes, she did not let you down like the others, but that was through no virtue of her own. She was dying. It's easy to be faithful when one has terminal cancer and one's lover is also her caregiver. Face it, Sydney: Everyone in town is aware of Brett's track record. She wasn't exactly long-term commitment material. A party girl, an easy lay..."

"Don't you dare speak of my Brett that way!"

"I know it hurts, Sydney, but you need to face facts: Under different circumstances, she, too, would have let you down. You need to learn not to be dependent on relationships."

"Brett loved me."

"Of course she did. You took care of her." Raevynn smirked, "You'll never be able to find out how it would've played out over time. I see a pattern here with all your relationships. They're idealized in your memory. Dead lovers in particular have the dubious honor of being immortalized as fairy tale characters. The message is clear: You are not meant to be with anyone. You need to accept that and get on with your mission in life."

"Everyone needs love, trust and a sense of belonging."

"It's important to overcome our needs and evolve to a higher plane. We all have to follow the path God has chosen for us."

"That does not necessarily have to exclude our loved ones."

"For some, it does. For you, it definitely does. You were meant to devote your life to doing God's work. Just an overview of your life and your personality makes it abundantly clear: You are meant to be the next Mother Theresa."

"Raevynn, I don't want to be a saint. I'm just an ordinary woman."

"There's nothing ordinary about you, Sydney. Living like other women is not in the cards for you. You must stop obsessing over trying to get your needs met. You have to think about other people. You need to sever your ties with all your toxic, clingy friends. They're keeping you stuck in unhealthy patterns. You need to make a clean break."

"They're my support system."

"You don't need them. You have me. They're just leeches."

"They've been with me through thick and thin."

"They have their personal agendas. They don't want you to grow. As long as you remain unhealthy, you provide what they need."

"They give more than they receive."

"Poor, misguided Sydney." Raevynn shook her head, "I have great visions of your future. I see you in a monastery, contented and fulfilled. That is your mission in life. You are going to find yourself so much at peace once you get on the right track and give up all your worldly possessions. You can't imagine how happy I feel now that I am doing what I was meant to do. The women in my collective and I have a sacred bond and a deep love. We're all friends, sisters and lovers. I have found my calling. You need to seek yours. You can start by giving away all your worldly possessions. I can help you with that. You can get much closer to God that way…Oh, look at the time! I have to go! Zilla's meeting me and we're going to see a play!"

*　*　*

Raevynn sauntered down Queen Street to Memorial Park, where Sydney was reading on a turquoise park bench beside the pond. The plump concrete beavers adorning the pond were painted the same garish shade of turquoise. Short and squat, Raevynn carried herself proudly, her oversized breasts unrestricted under her orange peasant blouse. Her protruding chin held high, she was licking an ice cream cone. Her long wild hair was pulled away from her face into a taut bun, exposing her ravaged complexion. She sat beside Sydney and leaned back.

"I'm giving another workshop for incest survivors in two weeks. I expect you to take care of all the arrangements: The advertising, refreshments and the space." she shoved the last piece of her ice cream cone into her mouth.

"Raevynn," Sydney peered into her face, forming her words cautiously, "I don't think that will be possible."

"You can't pull out now! You'd be letting down all those women who desperately need my help! You don't appreciate the work I'm doing."

"Raevynn, I can't."

"You're just like all the others. Selfish and ungrateful. Suit yourself, then."

"I'm sorry, I can't do this anymore. It's taking too much of a toll on me."

192

"I don't care. I certainly won't lose any sleep over it, but those poor women are going to miss out because of your selfishness."

"Maybe someone from your collective could provide some space."

"Your house is the perfect setting for it: A homey, non-threatening place, where the women could feel safe. You owe me a hundred dollars."

"For what?"

"For having to find an alternate location, for advertising, for refreshments, for my inconvenience. I was counting on you and you left me high and dry."

"Raevynn..."

"I'll give you a chance to come to your senses. You have until Thursday. If you don't come through for me, it's your loss, Missy. Looks like I was wrong about you. You're not such a beautiful person, after all. I'm sure those poor women will be pretty disgusted with you, too, when I tell them how you let them down. And, by the way, they're very homophobic. When they find out you're a lesbian, they'll put a collective curse on all your businesses. You'll be sorry you ever messed with me." Raevynn burst into laughter – fiendish, mad, bone-chilling laughter, her face grotesquely horrifying; she was slapping her knees and rocking back and forth.

"Good bye, Raevynn." Sydney rose.

"You can't live without me. You'll be begging me to come back. In Vancouver, people were breaking down my door for a chance to be my clients."

"That's because most people in Vancouver are stoned out of their minds." she retorted.

"You'll be sorry." Raevynn glared at her with narrow pinpoint eyes, "You'll never know what you missed. You could've had the world with me. But you chose smug middle-class conformity. You'll come to your senses someday, but it'll be too late by then."

Raevynn swept past her and across the street, leaving Sydney alone with tremors that shook her entire body. True to her name, Raevynn preyed on the wounded, the dying and the walking dead.

Chapter 22/ WHERE WOULD I BE?

From the dining room, he could see her rinsing the dishes and placing them carefully in the dishwasher. In her lilac chiffon dress, she appeared out of place.

"Never mind the dishes. Fred can clean up in the morning." he called out to her.

"Fred went to all this trouble to prepare this elegant dinner for us. The least I can do is clean up after us. And, besides, Fred's not coming in the morning." she called back.

"He's not?"

"I gave him the day off." she wiped her hands with a towel and joined him in the dining room with a mischievous smile.

"What are you up to, Stormy?" he smirked, shaking his head in disbelief.

"This." she bent down to kiss him, her tongue sweeping over his teeth and exploring the once-familiar caverns of his mouth; he responded instinctively, his tongue reaching desperately down her throat, sending shivers through her body.

"What are you doing?" he pulled away in sudden realization.

"What do you think I'm doing?" she kissed him again, savoring the lingering flavor of Crème Brule.

He was no longer putting up any resistance. She removed his tie and tossed it on the floor. He pulled her face down and kissed her long and hard. She was clutching his shirt. As he released her, his fingers brushed against her moist cheek. A slow smile spread across his face. She unbuttoned his shirt and bent down to kiss the smooth hair on his chest. Feeling his hands reaching under her dress, she moaned. His fingers vibrated against her sweet spot, sending her into violent spasms and shrieks of ecstasy. He pulled out his hand and licked his fingers. She led him down the hallway to the bedroom. Still trembling, she pulled off his now wrinkled burgundy shirt, removed his shoes and socks, unbuckled his belt and unzipped his fly. She stood before him, her eyes dark and lambent. He caressed her slowly and deliberately over her dress. He slid the straps of her dress down her shoulders to expose her breasts. Pulling her closer, he kissed her again, harder, more compelling, his tears mingling with hers. She wriggled out of her dress, slid off her panties and let them fall. He wheeled himself to the bed and locked the wheelchair. She turned down the covers. He rolled himself onto the bed. Climbing up beside him, she eased him out of his pants and shorts. Her fingers massaged his chest, moving lower with the gentlest touch. He closed his eyes and moaned. She took him in her hand and kissed it softly. She mounted him, guiding him inside her with her hand, slowly rotating her hips, working her way up to a rapid rhythm. He was squeezing her breasts. She lowered herself, allowing them to brush against his face. He at first suckled them, then, he bit them hard. Clutching his hair, she screamed in frenzy as he dissolved into her. Neither one spoke. She slid down and nestled beside him, her body moulding against his, both of them sticky. He placed an arm over her. She drifted off into a peaceful slumber. His eyes transfixed on the ceiling fan, he listened to her breathing. He did not move until the fingers of dawn crept in through the slats of the window blinds.

She stirred and opened her eyes.

"Good morning." she said groggily.

"Good morning, Stormy." he said, "Are you all right?"

"I'm great. How about you?"

"What do you think?" he winked, "What's going on, Stormy?"

"I don't know what you mean."

"What brought this on? What's wrong?"

"Does something have to be wrong for me to want to make love to you?"

"What do you think? I've been hitting on you for years and you've been brushing me off all this time. Now, all of a sudden, you're hot for me."

"I wanted to be with you, Warren. Why is that so wrong?"

"I've fantasized countless times about fucking you – but not like this."

"You mean not with me as the aggressor?"

"It's not like you, Stormy. You don't even like being on top. I know you too well. You can't fool me. What's going on?"

"Maybe I wanted to make love to the real Warren – not the one behind all the bravado."

"I thought you'd sworn off men."

"Only new men."

"So, old men are acceptable?" he laughed.

"In a manner of speaking."

"Aren't you supposed to be into chicks now?"

"No. Not before or since Brett."

"Stormy, Stormy, I can't keep up with you."

"Life is fragile, Warren. You've got to grab happiness when and where you find it." she stroked his cheek.

"You need to feel needed. You have a need to take care of all the broken people you meet. Now that I'm broken, you want to take care of me."

"It's not like that."

"Would you have come on to me if I weren't in this wheelchair?"

"Why are you questioning everything, Warren? Why can't you just let things be?"

"Because I'm not right for you, Sydney."

"Oh, it's Sydney now. That means you're serious."

"I am serious. You shouldn't be wasting your time with me. You should be out there, meeting other men."

"I've sworn off new men – remember?"

"Sydney Goldstein – what am I going to do with you?" he threw his hands up in the air.

"Just be here with me."

"As tempting as that sounds, I'd be taking advantage of you."

"You have my permission to take advantage of me."

"I think you're crazy."

"Crazy is good."

"In that case, how about a repeat performance? We're already naked and dirty."

"That's more like the Warren I know."

* * *

Daniel walked up the driveway to the small patio tucked behind the white bungalow.

"How's it going, buddy?" he called out to Warren, who was reading Time Magazine and listening to The Beach Boys song 'God Only Knows' on the ghetto blaster beside him on the side table, "I just got your message that you wanted to see me."

"Have a seat, Dan." he motioned toward the ornate white lawn chair nearby, "Would you like a beer? The door's not locked. Help yourself."

"No, thanks." he sat, leaning forward, "Eli said you wanted to talk to me. What about?"

"Sydney."

"Okay."

"How much do you know?"

"About what?"

"I gather she hasn't told you anything."

"Warren, you know I can't divulge anything Sydney tells me. But, what is this about?"

"I need you to convince her to stay away from me."

"Why would you say that? I thought the two of you were getting on famously. She considers you a dear friend. Has something happened?"

"You could say that." Warren took a swig from the beer bottle on his side table.

"Have you two quarreled?"

"No. Nothing like that."

"Okay, then. Can you enlighten me?"

"We had sex."

Daniel's eyes widened.

"Now, you can see why I want her to stay away from me."

"Were you the one who initiated it?"

"I know no one would ever believe this, but it was she."

"Wow. I should've taken you up on your offer of that beer."

"She hasn't been back since then. I think she has regrets. I can't say that I blame her. I didn't treat her right when we were dating years ago."

"That was nearly twenty years ago, Warren. You two are not the same people you were then. Both of you have evolved. You've moved beyond that tragic relationship and formed a strong bond. She's most likely still processing what happened. That might be why she hasn't been around."

"I've been hitting on her for years without any success. She's always wanted to maintain a platonic status. Then, right out of the blue, she comes on to me with unbridled passion."

"Sydney's a passionate, complex woman. Most heterosexual men would give their eyeteeth to trade places with you."

"Had this happened before my accident, I would've thought all my Christmases had arrived at once."

"Why is it different now?"

"I'm no good for her. I have to cut her loose before she's in too deep, before things get more complicated."

"Sydney apparently doesn't see it that way, or she wouldn't have initiated this new relationship with you."

"She shouldn't be wasting her time with me. She deserves better. She should be living her life to the fullest, meeting other people who are more suited for her."

"You know no one can tell Sydney what to do."

"I know how stubborn and strong-willed she is." he smiled wistfully.

"Have you tried talking to her about this?"

"Yes, but it's fallen on deaf ears."

"Maybe she knows exactly what she's getting into and she's prepared for the consequences. Give her some credit, pal."

"If I were the old me, I would've taken advantage of her, but I'm not that cad anymore."

"You care deeply about Sydney, don't you?"

"That's why I want to protect her from the likes of me."

"She obviously has deep feelings for you, too."

"I don't want her to have feelings for me. I don't deserve it."

"Whether or not you deserve it, she cares about you and you have to accept it. Just enjoy this second chance you've been given. Treat her right this time, now that you know better. Show her how special she is to you."

"You know, I've been with more women than I can even count. None of them meant anything to me. Then, I met Sydney...I didn't know what hit me. I couldn't deal with it, so I fucked it up royally."

"Are you afraid of losing her again?"

"If I allow myself to get pulled into the maelstrom, I might lose my mind. I don't know how to deal with this deep level of intimacy. It's so intense, it scares the hell out of me, man. I want her so much, I feel like my heart is going to explode. I've never experienced it with another woman. Sometimes, I think she's not of this world. Without a doubt, it's the most sacred blessing I've ever known and one I never imagined possible."

"Just be grateful for the gift you've been given, Warren. Treasure it and never let it go. Very few are that fortunate." Daniel rose, "Take care, man. I'm going to leave you with this for now, till next time." he shook his hand.

"Thanks, Dan. I appreciate it."

"Any time." he waved as he walked away.

* * *

He watched her flitting about like a distressed butterfly.

"Slow down, Stormy. Just watching you is making me dizzy."

"I've got to finish your bed bath and get you into your pajamas before I call a cab."

"Relax. I'm pretty sure Fred's been on to us for a while now. No need to go to such trouble to cover our tracks."

"All the same, we can still show some decorum. I don't want him to come here in the morning and find you naked and soiled."

"Soiled? Is that how you describe it?" he laughed.

"It was the only word I could think of."

"Come on. Come back to bed." he patted the spot she had vacated.

"Let me get this wash basin out of here." she disappeared into the bathroom.

Propped up in bed against pillows, he dried himself off with the towels she had provided. She

203

returned from the bathroom and slid on his underwear and pajama pants with swift efficiency,

"Good. Now, you're decent." she stood back, "And, I've got to get home."

"You don't have to leave. Why don't you stay the night?"

"I'd have to wake up and leave before Fred gets here."

"Don't worry. I'll be awake long before he gets here. I'll call and tell him to come later."

"In that case..."

"You can wear my pajama top. I don't want to be tempted and get 'soiled' again." he winked.

She smiled knowingly and put on the pajama top.

"It's so peaceful at night, with just the two of us." she propped herself up beside him.

He placed an arm around her and guided her head to his shoulder.

"Stormy...I need to talk to you..."

"Is something wrong?"

"No. Nothing like that. There are some things I need to tell you."

"Warren, you're scaring me."

"It's not anything to panic about. I don't have cancer or anything. There are some things from the past that I need to come clean about...things you have a right to know."

"Are they bad things?"

"It depends on your perspective."

"I'm listening."

"First, I have to warn you: There might be emotional triggers for you. If you feel overwhelmed, let me know."

She nodded.

"Going back to the night of the fire at the club...I don't know how much you remember...There are some things you don't know."

"My memory of that time is spotty at best."

"It was arson."

"I thought it was an electrical fire, caused by aluminum wiring."

"It was caused by a deliberate overloading of the circuits by the new maintenance man."

"Did they ever catch him?"

"No."

"Why did he do it? Does anyone know?"

"He was hired to do it."

"By whom?"

"Linda."

"Linda...Isn't she dead?"

"Yes."

"Why did she hire him to burn down the club?"

"Because she was blinded by her jealousy and rage that Jack chose you over her."

"It's scary what lengths some people are willing to go to for revenge."

"There is more to the story."

"I wonder how she died."

"I'll get to that...She ordered Larry to go to the hospital and kill you."

Her eyes grew in terror.

"He could not carry out his mission because he was killed."

"But they never found his body. They thought he skipped town."

"His killers were instructed to dispose of his body properly. They were pros."

"How do you know all this, Warren?"

"I'll get to that, too. Linda was killed by the same person who ordered the hit on Larry."

"Do you know who it is?"

"I do."

"Does anyone else know? Her murder's never been solved."

"No one else knows. When I reveal his identity, you and I are going to be the only ones who know. What you choose to do with the information is up to you. I think you have a right to know the truth."

She was trembling in his arms like a wounded sparrow.

"Yes, Stormy, I'm responsible for their deaths."

His lips taut, his brows furrowed, he was looking straight ahead. She glanced up at him with moist eyes and caressed his cheek.

"Thank you." she whispered, clasping his hand, "I love you, Warren."

"I love you, Stormy."

Chapter 23/ GRAB AND RUN

"None of this feels real. I feel I'm going to wake up any minute and find out it was all a dream, a beautiful dream, and you don't really exist." Jack's eyes panned the festive restaurant with painted wooden chairs in rainbow hues and strings of pastel colored lights forming canopies over the tables, "This can't be me, with the most beautiful woman in Istanbul, eating Al Fresco with a breathtaking view of the Bosphorus." he gazed across the road at the water glittering in the sunlight.

"Don't forget to turn your coffee cup upside down, so I can tell your fortune." Sureyya winked suggestively.

"I don't want to know if my fortune says this dream has to end."

"It doesn't have to end, Jack. You do not have to return to America with your friends at the end of six weeks. I'm sure there's some way you can arrange to live here permanently."

"I would love that."

"We could move to the other side of the Bosphorus."

"What's wrong with this side? It looks pretty nice to me."

"It's better on the other side. I'll take you there next week."

"Next week is good. I need time to recover from all our excursions this week...Topkapi Palace, Grand Bazaar...My feet are still sore. I don't know how you can still walk after being on your feet all that time with those heels.”

“You get used to it when you live here.”

“What's on the other side that you can't find here?”

“More nostalgia. It's not as nice as it used to be, but it holds a special place in my heart. There were so many beautiful beaches when I was a little girl, but they filled in the sea and paved over the beaches.”

“Are you serious? Why would they do that?”

“I don't know. They filled in the sea on this side, too, in Arnavutkoy. There were houses built right by the water. They filled in the sea and put in a road in front of the houses.”

“That's interesting. What happened to all the beaches on the other side?”

“All gone. My entire childhood was spent there. Now, all I have are memories.”

“I'm sorry.”

“There used to be a beach named after me.”

“A beach named after you?”

“Yes. Sureyya Beach. It had a gorgeous monument in the middle of the water. People could swim to it. The sand was like white silk. The water was so warm, almost purple, crystal clear, with soft sand under your feet.”

“Sounds incredible.”

“I swam to that monument every morning when I was little.”

"Did they really name it after you?"

"I'm just pulling your foot."

"You mean my leg." he laughed.

"It really was named Sureyya Beach, though. I thought I'd joke with you."

"You got me. I'd love to go across the Bosphorus with you to see where the beaches were."

"That monument's sitting in the little park beside the parking lot of a supermarket in Maltepe now."

"Do you have any pictures from when you were a kid?"

"Only a few. My father left us before I started school. No one took my pictures after that."

"I'm sorry."

"He disappeared. He didn't want a family."

"Do you have any brothers or sisters?"

"No. Even one child was too many for him."

"Sureyya, that's so sad. I'm so sorry you went through that."

"I got used to it. My mother went to work after he left us. I hardly ever saw her. She was never home at nights. Our neighbors took care of me. We were so poor, she couldn't afford wood for the stove, so we had no heat. There was never any food. I promised myself I'd never live like that again when I grew up."

"You mentioned once that you were married at one time. Were you happy?"

"I thought I would be, but it didn't live up to my expectations."

"You don't have to worry about anything anymore." he reached across the table and held her hand.

"You're the nicest man I've ever met, Jack. But your friends don't like me very much, do they?"

"Don't worry about them."

"How did you get to be friends with them? They are homosexual, but you like the ladies."

"It's a long story. They're the best friends a guy could ever ask for. They've been there for me through my darkest days."

"You're a man of mystery, Jack. That makes you even more exciting."

"I think you're the mysterious one."

"I guess we both have our sorrows and secrets...Come on, finish your coffee and turn it over. It must be cold by now."

"That's okay. I love cold coffee."

"I'll make you a fresh one back at my apartment."

"That might keep me up all night. Turkish coffee is pretty strong." he took his last sip.

"I'll show you how to turn it over." she took his cup, placed the saucer over it, turned it over in one swift movement, and rotated it a few times, "Make a wish. Press your index finger on the top if your wish is business related, and press your ring finger if it's matters of the heart."

"What if it's both?"

"You have to choose one."

He pressed his ring finger over it and made a silent wish.

"Now, we have to wait for it to settle." she said.

"This meal's been fabulous. It's amazing that you folks grill and serve your fish with the head and the tail intact. It's so delicious that way, you don't even need anything to add to it...And, those appetizers and side dishes were out of this world...I love those pastries...And the cake...It had pistachios in it. You're so fortunate to be living here."

"You could be living here, too, if you want to." she picked up his coffee cup and gazed into it intently, "Your fortune is very good. You're going to have a financial windfall. Many open roads await you. You have upcoming celebrations and merriment. I also see a marriage in your future, Jack...A woman with a lot of curves."

"I think I'm looking at her."

"I see some sort of a trinket, something shiny next to this woman."

"A present I might be buying." he winked.

"I see a lot of happiness and celebration. It's a very good fortune." she put down the cup, "Maybe we ought to get going." she retrieved her lightweight cream-colored leather jacket from the back of her blue-painted wooden chair.

Jack glanced at the check, and reached for his wallet. He carefully removed the required amount of bills and added one for the gratuity.

"Garcon!" he called out to their waiter, who was serving shish-kabobs three tables away.

When he arrived at their table, the young man said something in Turkish, to which Sureyya nodded "yes". Once he was gone, she stood and took Jack's arm. They descended the concrete steps to the sidewalk.

"We can take a grab and run. It would be faster." she led him to the edge of the sidewalk.

"Grab and run?"

"They're little buses that come around more frequently, get filled up faster, and take you home in record time."

"Sounds good to me."

A beat-up brown van reminiscent of the iconic VW hippie vans of the sixties stopped in front of them. She motioned to him to follow her in. He produced change from his pocket and held it out in his palm. She selected the required amount for their fare and led him to the two unoccupied seats at the back, covered in zebra print plush. The other passengers appeared to be mostly young men in suits and elderly women in floral dresses with shopping bags. He smiled awkwardly. The women smiled back and nodded. One of them murmured something in Turkish. He remembered to say: "Thank you, Auntie." In Turkish.

"She said: 'May God protect you from the evil eye, my son.'." Sureyya whispered.

Then, the woman said something to Sureyya.

"She said: 'Your partner looks like a door. May God bless you both.'" she told him.

"A door?"

"It means tall and handsome."

"That's quite an unusual analogy. I like it." he settled back in his seat to enjoy the lush scenery from the window, his hand linked with Sureyya's.

* * *

"Fancy seeing you here." Aydin playfully tapped Jack's arm, "Did you and Sureyya have a lovers' tiff? You haven't been to breakfast with us since you met her. To what do we owe this honor?"

"Sureyya had a doctor's appointment first thing this morning, so she had to get to bed at a decent time."

"You may want to do the same." Kent said solemnly.

"Get to bed early?" Jack appeared perplexed.

"No. Go to a doctor."

"Why? I feel great."

"You need to go for a different reason."

"I don't have any reason to see a doctor."

"You need to be tested for STDs, bud." Aydin said.

"You think so?"

"Yeah. What do you think? They don't call her Surtuk Sureyya for nothing."

"But..."

"Surely, you didn't think you were the only one...This is Sureyya we are talking about, bud. Not some nice divorced or widowed lady with a couple of kids who only dates respectable men."

"With so many gorgeous and respectable ladies around, you pick the one Trollope in the bunch." Kent said.

"She sort of picked me."

"What does that tell you?"

"You two really think I need to be tested for STDs?"

"Definitely."

"I'll do it, just so I can prove to you that Sureyya is clean."

"If that's what it takes to get you to a doctor, I'm fine with that." Kent said, "I hope you're right and we're wrong. But, to be on the safe side, after this, you really should practice safe sex; use a condom."

"That would hurt her feelings. She'd know I didn't trust her."

"Of course, her feelings are so much more important than your health."

"Cut her some slack, guys. She's had a rough childhood."

Aydin and Kent mimicked playing the violin.

"Her dad abandoned her as a child. Her mother raised her alone. They were so poor, they couldn't afford food or firewood."

"Her mother worked in a brothel to support her." Kent said.

"How do you know?"

"It's well-known around here."

"Maybe she had no other skills. I'm glad Sureyya didn't follow in her footsteps."

"At least, brothels are legal. They are registered as businesses and pay taxes. The ladies are tested regularly for STDs. But Sureyya is freelancing. No mandatory testing. You have no idea where she's been. The ladies at the brothels have no pretense. They don't claim to be anything else. But Sureyya is the queen of deception."

"I'm sure you two are overreacting, but I'll get tested. Why don't we get in line for the breakfast buffet? I can hear those stuffed grape leaves calling out to me."

"I can get you in to see a doctor this afternoon." Kent said, as they lined up behind a group of morose business people in suits, "He's my uncle's friend, and his office is in Yenikoy, which is nearby. I'll call him after breakfast. He can speed up the process and get the results very quickly. But, for Pete's Sake, Jack, keep your pants on in the next little while. Tell her you've come down with the flu or something – anything – to keep your distance."

* * *

"Go ahead and say 'I told you so.'" Jack sat at the edge of his bed, "Three STDs. I never thought it would happen to me. Chlamydia, Gonorrhoea, Trichomoniasis."

"We're not going to say 'I told you so', Jack. We're relieved you're getting treated."

"I know you want me to stay away from her from now on. I just don't know how to break it to her."

"Never in my wildest dreams," Aydin laughed, "Did I imagine I'd be giving advice to a straight man about women."

"Neither did I." Kent said.

"I have to say goodbye to her."

"Can you do it without jumping in the sack?" Kent smirked.

"You know, she told my coffee fortune. She saw a wedding with me and a curvy woman...and shiny jewellery."

"And you believed her?" Kent shook his head.

"Tell you what, Jack." Aydin said, "You take it easy while you're on those antibiotics. When you feel better, go see her and tell her we're all leaving early because you've got some medical issue. Be as vague as possible."

"For now, get some rest. Don't fret about it. Get yourself healthy. It'll all work out in the end."

Chapter 24/ AUGUST WINDS

Leaves of gold and brown, curling inward like a child's fingers clutching stolen candies, crackled under his wheelchair. The maples along The Green had resigned themselves to shedding their leaves. Summer was coming to a close. He locked his wheelchair. She sat on the bench beside him.

"August is the saddest month." she sighed.

"It's summer's death."

"As she takes her last breath, she still tries so hard to warm us."

"Autumn is merciless."

"Autumn bursts on the scene, pushes summer out of the way and takes charge...I can't bear to see the fallen leaves."

"August winds are harbingers of death." he stared ahead at the river.

Struck by an inexplicable sense of loss, she stood and wound her arms tightly around him.

"What's this about?" he looked up at her.

"I needed to feel you close to me."

"You're such an enigma, you know that?" he squeezed her hand.

"Warren?" she returned to her seat.

"Hmmm?"

"There's something I need to tell you, too."

"From the look on your face, I get the feeling it's not good."

She gazed up at him with frightened eyes.

"Hit me with it, Stormy."

"My pregnancy way back in '76...You were convinced the baby I miscarried was yours."

"And you insisted it was the product of a one night stand in Toronto."

"You didn't believe me."

"I didn't believe it then, and I don't believe it now. I can't see you engaging in anonymous sex with a stranger."

"It wasn't a stranger. But the baby was conceived in Toronto. I'm sorry for the grief I caused you by not disclosing the identity of the father. Too many innocent people would've been hurt if I had."

"Go on. Tell me now."

"It was Jacob."

"Jacob? Your cousin Jacob?"

She nodded. His eyes were distant and weary.

"You had a right to know. I'm sorry."

"I'm sorry, too. For everything that went down back then. Let's go home, Stormy." he reached out for her hand.

"Yes, let's go home."

*　*　*

The persistent ringing of the doorbell awakened her. She bolted out of bed, hastily put on her robe and ran down the stairs, with her sash hanging loose. Eli and Daniel were at her door.

"I'm sorry to wake you up at this ungodly hour, Syd, but something's happened." Eli said as they stepped into the vestibule.

"What's happened?"

"You need to sit down first." Daniel led her to the living room sofa, "It's Warren."

"What's wrong with Warren? Is he in the hospital? I'll get dressed, so we can go see him."

"Sydney," Eli sat beside her and held her shoulders, "I'm afraid Warren's gone."

"No. He can't be gone. I just saw him last night. He was fine."

"He had a heart attack in his sleep. Fred found him this morning." Daniel sat on the other side of her.

"No. It can't be...I should've been there with him...I came home last night because he had an early appointment with a specialist. I wanted him to be well rested for it. The doctor was going to discuss a new therapy with him. He was quite hopeful he would be able to regain the use of his legs...I should've been there beside him. He shouldn't have died alone."

"Don't do this to yourself, Sydney." Eli held her; her tears fell on his green cotton shirt.

"He loved you very much, Sydney. Warren and I had some long talks." Daniel said.

"And I loved him."

"He knew that. He was grateful to have you in his life."

"Fate had just led us back to each other. We were building a whole new relationship – this time, the right way."

"And, he found tremendous strength in his relationship with you."

"Fate is cruel. We had so little time…We were led back to each other, only to be torn apart again."

"But the time you had was very special. No one can take that away from you."

"All I have left now are memories…of Jack, Tony, Brett, my parents, Marin and Brettiella, and now Warren…Everyone I love either dies or goes away. I hope I don't live long enough for you two and the girls to become memories, too."

"Don't worry. We're not going anywhere. You'll never be able to get rid of us." Daniel winked.

She smiled.

"I'll call your doctor to see if he can phone in a prescription for you." Daniel offered, "I can pick it up and bring it here."

"No. No meds." she shook her head emphatically.

"Are you sure? You feel things so strongly. I'm worried about you, Syd."

"I'm sure. I don't want a crutch."

"Everyone needs a little help at times."

"I'll be okay."

"She's a strong lady." Eli said.

"I have to see Dottie. I have to help with the funeral arrangements. She can't be in any condition to take it all on."

"It's all right. Peggy and Maxine are helping her."

"She must be devastated."

"Don't worry: Peggy, Maxine and Olga are there for her. Peggy called us and asked us to tell you in person. They didn't want you to find out over the phone."

"I'm going to miss him so much..."

"Listen, pretty lady, since you don't want any meds, I'm going to bring you a bottle of brandy."

"That's kind of you, Daniel, but I hardly ever drink nowadays. When Brett got sick, we both quit alcohol and coffee. I seldom touch either one even now. One coffee in the morning, and the odd martini on special occasions, but, even then, I usually stick with Club Soda...I'll be all right I promise."

"You drive a hard bargain. We're going to fix your dinner tonight and bring it here to eat with you."

"You don't have to go to so much trouble. I'm not going to have much of an appetite."

"That's why we're going to be here to force-feed you."

"What would I ever do without you two?"

Overcome by sudden emotion, she opened her arms to enclose them both.

*　*　*

She awoke to the faint sensation of a hand on her shoulder.

"Stormy..." she heard a soft whisper.

"Warren?"

"I don't want you to grieve for me, Stormy. Move on with your life. That's what I want for you. As summer takes her last breath, look for me in the August Winds. That's where I'll be."

Chapter 25/ AT THE END OF OUR LOVE AFFAIR

Jack rang her buzzer repeatedly, all to no avail. He then stood under her balcony, shouting out her name. Halit, the elderly neighbor, came outside, waving his arms, speaking in a panicked tone, desperately attempting to communicate. Jack pulled out a small notepad and a pen from an inside pocket and handed them to Halit. The older man's eyes sparkled as he hastily drew a stick woman and wrote "Sureyya" over her head. He proceeded to draw a stick man and wrote "Fikret" over his head. He drew a plus sign between the two figures.

"Are they married?" Jack asked weakly.

Halit shook his head in confusion. Jack pointed to his left ring finger. When Halit shook his head "no", Jack smiled in relief. An older woman with a blonde bob and bifocals, wearing a cobalt blue business suit emerged from the building and exchanged greetings with Halit. He said something to her, casting a glance toward Jack. He heard "America", and Sureyya's name.

"Hello." the woman spoke to Jack in English.

"Hello. I'm Jack."

"Welcome to our city, Jack Bey. I'm Feyza. Halit Bey asked me to help you. I speak English."

"Thank you. That's a relief." he put his notebook and pen back in his pocket, "Thank you, Halit Bey." he turned to the man, who smiled and waved goodbye as he entered the building.

"Let's walk down the street a little bit." Feyza said, "Halit Bey said you were looking for Sureyya. I'll explain everything to you."

Jack followed her to the main road, where they crossed over to the paved area by the seashore with benches and food carts.

"Would you like a simit?" he asked her as they sat on a bench beside the red and white cart with thin, doughy rings covered in sesame seeds on display.

"That's very kind of you."

He bought two simits and handed one to her.

"Thank you. I understand you've become friends with our Sureyya, Jack Bey; am I right?"

"Yes. I came to say goodbye to her this morning. My friends and I are returning home tomorrow. She wouldn't buzz me in, or even come out to the balcony to speak to me. Then, Halit Bey drew me a stick figure of Sureyya next to a stick figure of a man."

"Ah, yes, Fikret."

"He indicated they were not married. Is this Fikret her sugar daddy?"

"I don't understand: Sugar Daddy?"

Jack reached in his pocket for his tiny English-Turkish dictionary and searched frantically.

"*Seker Baba!*" he called out proudly.

"*Seker Baba*? A father who gives out candy? An older gentleman who gives candy to children? Like *Noel Baba*?"

"No, no. Not like *Noel Baba*. A sugar daddy is a man with financial means who takes care of a lady in exchange for you know what."

"I see now. Yes. Fikret is her sugar daddy. He's a businessman. He travels frequently. Jack Bey, I don't want to be impolite, but Sureyya is not a suitable companion for you."

"It's not impolite at all. Thank you for caring. Does this Fikret have any idea Sureyya has other gentleman friends?"

"I'm sure he does."

"And, he puts up with it?"

"Puts up? I'm not sure I understand."

"Tolerates."

"Yes, he tolerates it. He has a wife and children himself, so he can't complain. They fight every time he returns from a business trip. I'm sorry you were hurt by her scheming, selfish ways. I can tell you are a kind, caring gentleman. Other tourists enjoy themselves with her while they are on holidays here and when they go home, they forget about her. I can tell you have formed an attachment to her. It's good that you are returning home."

"I'm a big fool."

"No. You are a decent human being."

"Thank you, Mrs. Feyza. I've already taken up too much of your time. You were on your way some place. I hope I didn't keep you from something you had to do."

"I'm going to visit a former colleague who is not feeling well. There are some very good bakeries on the way. I thought I'd buy some sweets to cheer her up."

"I hope she feels better soon."

"Thank you. We worked together for thirty-five years as marine biologists. We retired at the same time. She's a very dear friend."

"Thank you for talking to me, Mrs. Feyza."

"Good luck to you. I hope you and your friends have a safe trip home." she stood and smoothed out her skirt before embarking on her mission.

Alone by the seashore, Jack bought himself another simit and broke off small pieces to share with the seagulls. This city of unsurpassed beauty would soon become only a memory. A calico cat was rubbing against his ankles. He broke off more pieces from his simit and placed them on the ground for her. The cat glanced up at him, imploring to be picked up. He gathered her up and caressed her warm fur. They sat together, watching the fishermen's boats and the elaborately designed ferries carrying passengers back and forth across the Bosphorus. He remained long after the cat jumped off his lap and wandered away in search of new friends. He was alone. He would always be alone with this emptiness in his soul. His love affair with Sureyya had come to an end, but his love affair with Istanbul would never end.

Chapter 26/ WITCHES, GOBLINS, AND GHOSTS

She stood on her front porch, her arms folded across her chest. Exuberant children in polyester costumes scuttled off, the girls' candy-colored princess gowns dragging on the sidewalk. Their innocent chatter faded away. Distant sirens stabbed at her heart. Shivering in her turtleneck, she returned inside, turned off the porch light and locked her door. The sirens persisted. She filled her tea kettle and plugged it in. Eli knocked at her kitchen door. He was wearing a Dracula costume. She burst into laughter as she opened the door.

"You're just in time for tea." she said, "The trick-or-treaters must've loved your costume."

"Especially all the fellow Draculas." he took a chair at the table, "Did you close up shop for the night?"

"There haven't been too many kids in the past half hour. I don't feel too comfortable after 8:30. Once the little ones go home, all the high school and university students come out, drunk and stoned from partying, with mischief on their minds. Living downtown can be unnerving on Halloween."

"We're right next door. We'll protect you."

"A few minutes ago I heard some sirens and it got me so spooked."

"There's always some sort of vandalism on Halloween. Some of those crazy university students are burning couches in the middle of the streets up the hill."

"I dread Halloween every year. It's sinister, downright demonic."

"I don't like it, either. Just an antiquated Pagan tradition that has become larger than life because of commercialism. Now, they even have Halloween lights and decorations. When we were kids, we made our own costumes out of castoffs."

"I remember cutting holes in old sheets for ghost costumes." she unplugged the tea kettle and poured water into the robin blue ceramic teapot.

"I remember wearing my dad's old clothes for hobo costumes."

"I was a witch or an old lady after I outgrew the ghost idea. I wore Donna's old dresses, fashioned witches' hats out of bristol board and carried old brooms." she poured tea into two blue mugs.

"Kids now have shiny, ready-made, store-bought costumes. What's the fun in that?"

"I hear sirens again, Eli. They sound like they're downtown, no going up the hill."

"I agree. They're somewhere nearby."

The ringing of the wall phone behind her caused her to jump.

"Sydney," Maxine's voice was on the other end, "There's something I need to tell you."

"Maxi, is it one of you girls? Are you all right?"

"It's nothing like that. But it's really bad."

Sydney's heart missed a beat. She was clutching the receiver tightly.

"It's the guest house...Mr. Horncastle's place."

"Has it been vandalized?"

"No. Much worse. It's on fire."

The receiver fell out of Sydney's hand. Eli caught it in midair with his right hand and supported her with his left arm around her.

"Maxine, it's me, Eli. What's going on? Are you ladies all right?"

"We're fine, Eli. But the guest house is on fire. It's pretty bad."

"Sydney and I are on our way. Thanks for letting us know, Maxine." he hung up the phone, "Syd, honey, do you think you'll be able to go there?"

She nodded.

"Let's get your coat and pocketbook, then."

He locked the door behind them and called out to Daniel to open their door.

"Warren's place is on fire. Syd and I are going there now. Can you hold down the fort here?"

"Sure thing. I'm sorry, Syd."

Eli bucked her seatbelt for her and drove as fast as speed limits would allow. Waterloo Row was blocked to traffic. He had to take a detour and park on University Avenue. They walked down Shore Street and turned the corner. The flames were shooting up past the trees, painting the sky a putrid orange. Billowing black smoke filled the air. The spectators screamed as a new explosion began consuming the rear portion. The stench of burning wood and burning plastic was choking them.

"The back part's about to blow!" someone called out.

"She's goin' up fast. Stand back." another man remarked.

The windows shattered one by one, spewing out chards of glass. And, there was a deafening boom as the bungalow folded into itself. The ground beneath Sydney's feet gave way. The voices and the roar of the raging blaze grew distant...Across the street, Helen and Hilda were shivering in their robes with curlers in their hair.

"Ain't no surprise to me." Helen said, "That family's cursed."

"I hear Warren Horncastle's been hauntin' the place. People've seen 'im in the windows when they were walkin' by. This could send Dorothy 'round the bend."

"All them people are touched in the head."

"That Stanley's a black widow. One dead husband, one dead fella, one dead gal, one missing ex-husband. She ain't gonna be gettin' asked out on too many dates."

Both of them chuckled.

The spectators remained until the fire department doused the remaining flare-ups. The once pristine white clapboard siding now lay charred in the rubble. A group of elderly men paused to survey the damage.

"I reckon they done it for insurance, Harry." one man said.

"Them rich folks is always burnin' down their buildings for insurance."

"That old cabin...Why, it's been just a sittin' empty all this time, and all the bills pilin' up at the big house...So, they done burnt down the little house."

"Maybe one of them ghosts done it." another man flashed a toothless grin, "My missus sez there's ghosts there. She seen Warren Horncastle's ghost."

"His missus never been all there. A few bricks short of a load." another man laughed.

"Yeah. Her elevator don't reach the top floor."

"There's been a rash of unexplained fires around the city in recent months." a younger woman in a navy blue Far West jacket remarked, "Most of them are centred around the university and the streets around it. One graduate student set fire to his professor's office and the library."

"He was a psych student, wasn't he, Roxanne? He's been apprehended, but there are a lot of other fire bugs out there. Beavertown is the fire capital of the country. I even heard it on the radio." another younger woman in a fuchsia Far West jacket said.

"Them psycho students is a menace!" one woman said, "They done set fire to Grace Mulholland's real estate sign on King's College Road. No wonder they want to move."

"I still say Warren Horncastle's the one who done it." another woman said.

"I've heard about him." the woman in fuchsia said, "He sounds like Heathcliff from Wuthering Heights...I heard he's been so consumed by his love for Sydney Goldstein all these years that he could not envision a life without her...Then, by the time she returned to him, he was disabled...He cannot accept the fact that he is dead now and cannot be with her anymore...Such a tragic love story."

"It ain't no love story, Paula." Helen said, "That woman never loved 'im. She was one of them lesbians. Got shacked up with a perfessor's ex-wife."

"I think she's bisecular." Hilda said.

"It ain't bisecular, dear." Helen said, "It's trisexual."

"It's bisexual." Paula corrected them.

"Them rich folks is always a messin' 'round with lotsa people, jumpin' into bed with all 'n sundry. Man, woman, beast – they don't care."

"Warren Horncastle was a tortured soul, not the heartless satyr everyone makes him out to be." Roxanne said, "Both the Horncastles and the Goldsteins have had so much tragedy in their lives. I hope that Sydney Goldstein can pick the pieces and get on with her life."

"I'm ashamed of all you folks revelling in other people's pain." Paula said.

"Well, la-di-da." Helen laughed, "Miss High 'N Mighty don't approve of us!"

Paula and Roxanne walked away from the crowd toward the gas station at the other end of Waterloo Row.

"Okay, folks," a middle-aged man spoke up, "There's nothing more to see here. Time to go home. Have some respect for the family."

Amid groans and snickers, the crowd dispersed. The stench of destruction hung heavy in the cold air as Sydney and Dottie huddled together.

* * *

"Hey, Serra, you're closing up tonight!" a young man with blemished skin taunted the young woman with the beaded cornbraids, "I'm glad I'm not you!"

She stuck her tongue out at him.

"Is it always this crazy on Halloween?" she asked Cleo, who was smiling knowingly.

"Pretty crazy, but not this bad. Don't worry: I'll stay with you and I'll take you home afterward. There's no way I'm leaving you alone and letting you take a cab home on a night like this."

"What a night. There were some women coming up to me complaining that there was a man in the ladies' washroom ogling them. I went down with Patrick to check, but we didn't find anybody there. I don't know if one of the customers was playing a prank."

"I think I have an idea who it might be." Cleo said.

"They described him as a middle-aged man in a suit."

"Yep. That's Warren Horncastle's ghost."

"Ghost? For real?"

"He likes to show up here once in a while."

"Wasn't he old, though, when he died?"

"Ghosts always look like the younger version of the person."

"Being a ghost must be the best anti-aging treatment."

Cleo let out a hearty laugh. Unaware of the humor in her own remark, Serra remained solemn.

"Why was he here when his house was burning down up the street? Shouldn't he be there?"

"I guess ghosts don't follow the same logic the living do."

"I hope he tracks down the scum that set his house on fire and haunts him."

"I have no doubt he will."

"What a strange night. I hope we never have another night like this again. Patrick had to break up so many brawls. The lights kept flickering. Some of the customers said they saw a very pretty brunette sitting at the bar asking for "one more martini" through the whole evening, but no one saw her actually drinking one, or the bartender serving her. Some of the men tried asking her to dance, but she didn't notice them."

"That would be Brett Morrow."

"The singer who used to work here?"

"Yes. She often hangs around the dressing room and the office, too."

"Wow. Now I understand why people keep quitting their jobs at this club. It must be bad for business, too, when you have ghosts in here."

"Actually, it seems to attract more people – just a different sort from the ones we used to get. In fact, a better sort."

"Cleo, I've checked all the stuff up here. I'm gonna split now." the young man with acne said, "Good night, ladies!"

"Thank you, Matt. See you tomorrow." Cleo said, "Let's do a walkthrough."

"The basement is really creepy." Serra followed Cleo tentatively.

They checked the dressing rooms, offices, bathrooms, and the utility room.

"We're done here." Cleo started back up the stairs.

"How does Sydney feel about owning a haunted club?"

"I think it's comforting for her."

"Not me. It gives me the heebie-jeebies."

"Seraphina Williams, you ain't seen nothing yet!" Cleo led her back into the darkened main lounge.

Against the moonlit backdrop, couples in formal attire were dancing to smooth piano music. Peter Nero's "Too Late Now" concluded and his "Wasn't The Summer Short?" began to play. As Cleo and Serra entered, the women in diaphanous gowns and their dance partners faded away. The lone figure at the bar remained, asking for "one more martini".

"I think I've seen enough." Serra turned to leave.

"Good night, Brett." Cleo whispered and followed Serra to the hallway.

"Does this happen often?" Serra asked.

"Every night after the customers leave."

"And it doesn't bother you?" Serra turned out the lights.

"Why would it? A visit from the other side is a blessing." Cleo locked the door behind them.

Chapter 27/ MUSIC FROM ACROSS THE WAY

"Agatha Christie slept here." his dinner companion said, "That's why they named the restaurant after her."

"Pera Palace Hotel…"he glanced around the restaurant, "It's magnificent…And, what a rich history it has. I'm glad you chose it."

"I like the central location. I know it's extravagant to stay at a luxury hotel, but I don't get to visit Istanbul too often. I wanted to make the most of this visit."

"I don't blame you. You need a little extra pampering after what Ebru did."

"When she pulled that stunt on me at the last minute like that, I was absolutely gutted."

"No wonder: You two plan this trip for months, she tells you to buy the tickets…Then, she breaks up with you and doesn't reimburse you for her ticket…That's brutal. You're better off without her."

"I'm very grateful to you, Jack. You really came through for me."

"Don't mention it, Ayla."

"I don't know what I would've done with that extra ticket I couldn't use, and being out all that money. If you hadn't bought Ebru's ticket from me, I would've had to stay at a youth hostel or something."

"It's a win-win. I couldn't believe I was being given another chance to visit Istanbul only four months after my last visit."

"This is a great location for shopping and night life. Beyoglu is the business district, the heart of the city. Anything you can't find in the rest of the city, you'll find here."

"Shopping and night life don't really hold much allure for me, Ayla, but this building is the perfect place to do some soul-searching. I feel Istanbul is my soul's home...It has some answers I'm seeking."

"I hope you find your answers, Jack."

"I feel a sense of belonging here...especially in this century-old hotel...It's almost as though I've been here before...It feels eerily familiar with its Neo Classical and Art Nouveau architecture and sumptuous décor."

"You might've stayed here when you were touring back in the seventies."

"I must have."

"This country was so blissfully liberal before the eighties. Once the right wing party came into power, it was the beginning of the end."

"The country's in a precarious position geographically, straddling two continents, embracing two opposing cultures."

"It's unique, but also tragic...I know this is changing the subject, but, I hope we get a chance to visit Galata Tower. It's a refurbished historic structure. There are shops on the main level. The upper levels have a coffee shop, a restaurant, a night club, and a balcony with a panoramic view of the city.

Don't worry: There are two elevators; you don't have to climb stairs."

"Sounds intriguing. By the way, they're playing some interesting music. Who's singing?"

"Zeki Muren: The most accomplished, celebrated, award-winning singer, composer and actor of all time and highly esteemed philanthropist. He never tried to conceal his sexual orientation. He did not openly declare he was gay, but made no attempt to project a heterosexual image, either. It had no impact on his career or his following. Not like Hollywood, where being openly gay has been the kiss of death for actors. But, the way things are going with one right wing government after another, this country is headed for doom."

"I hope not."

"When I was growing up, people from every religion, ethnicity and color co-existed in harmony throughout the city. It can never be like that again for the newer generations."

"The world was a kinder, gentler place back then."

"Right wing bullies are like rabid dogs, spreading hate and intolerance."

"I agree."

"I'm sorry. I'm ironing your head."

"Ironing my head?" he laughed, "I hope you got all the wrinkles out."

"Sorry."

"No, it's perfectly okay. You're not boring me at all. I love hearing everything about this magical, mystical city."

"I really hope you find the answers you're looking for here, Jack."

"Thanks, Ayla. And, I hope you find some healing and comfort, being here in your place of birth."

* * *

"There she is!" Ayla jumped up from her seat and started running toward the woman at the entrance, whose eyes were scanning the tea lounge.

They embraced and kissed each other on both cheeks, as was customary between friends. As they made their way back to the table, Jack rose to shake hands with Ayla's friend.

"Suzi, this is my friend Jack. And, Jack, this is my old childhood pal and partner in crime, Suzi."

"Very pleased to meet you." Jack shook her hand.

"Likewise." she smiled, and took a chair across from him, "It's getting quite cold out there."

"Istanbul winters can be brutal." Ayla sat beside Suzi, "Most days are damp and overcast. They chill you to the bone."

"Do you get much snow?" Jack asked.

"A light coating of a few inches around late January or February. It's quite pretty, really. But it melts in a few days."

"I hope you get warmed up after some tea and pastries." Jack said to Suzi.

"I'm sure I will." she smiled, "So, are you two boyfriend girlfriend?"

Ayla turned to him with terror in her eyes. Apparently, she had not disclosed her orientation to her friend.

"Yes." he stated firmly, his hand closing on hers, "I wanted to see the city where my girlfriend was born."

"That's very sweet." Suzi appeared amused, "Are you taking him to all the hot spots?" she asked Ayla.

"We're not much for the night life. We prefer quiet activities, like sightseeing, museums and such."

"You've done really well for yourself, Ayla. He's very impressive."

"Thanks." Ayla murmured, fidgeting with her napkin.

"I'm starting to feel warmer already." Suzi unbuttoned her navy wool coat and untied the red and gold acetate scarf wound round her neck. The flash of gold concealed behind the scarf, now glimmered under the bright overhead lights.

Jack's eyes were transfixed on the familiar symbol.

"Your necklace..." he stammered.

"Oh, yes. My Star Of David."

"It's exquisite."

"Thank you. If you want to know where you can get one for Ayla, don't bother. She's not Jewish." she winked at Ayla.

"There's...something very familiar about it..."he said.

"I'm sure a lot of Jewish women wear them in New York, as well." Suzi laughed.

He had not become that well-acquainted with or stood in close enough proximity to any Jewish women in New York to have noticed them wearing a Star Of David necklace...Yet...something about it was warm and comforting. His head was spinning. Fragments of songs began playing in his mind, overpowering the piped in "Beyond The Sea". He shut his eyes and held his head in his hands. Distant whispers and laughter echoed in his ears. He covered them in vain to shut out the noise.

"Your boyfriend looks distracted. He must be reminiscing about an old flame." Suzi's laughter rang out, piercing his eardrums.

He picked at the knees of his pants in an attempt to soothe the carpet burn he was suddenly feeling. He was on a carpet...an industrial carpet – on top of a woman...His head was nestled between her breasts.

"I've never loved anyone the way I love you." he was saying to her.

"I never imagined anything this beautiful was even humanly possible." she was murmuring.

He lifted his head to kiss her breasts. Two delicate gold chains were around her neck, their gold pendants concealed, hanging to one side. His fingers instinctively moved them back to the front. One was a heart locket, and the other...a Star Of David.

"Please excuse me." he stood up, hanging on to the side of the table for support, "I don't feel well. I'm sorry."

He made his way to the elevators and pressed the button with urgency. James Last's "Music From Across The Way" was being piped in. During the ride up to his room, the Star Of David was shimmering and whirling around him. He held onto the wall to steady himself.

"They'd have to knock me unconscious to pry it loose from me..." she was saying, lying in bed beside him, "I never intend to take it off. It symbolizes the persecution, suffering, perseverance and ultimate triumph of my people. It's my symbol of eternal hope."

He staggered out of the elevator and passed well-dressed couples in the corridor eyeing him with disdain before finding refuge in his room. He was going home. Yes, home. Where he belonged.

Chapter 28/ ALL THAT MY HEART CAN HOLD

The taxi rounded the corner to Waterloo Row. The driver cursed under his breath and opened the window to shout at a driver making an illegal turn.

"Hey, watch it, pal!" he closed the window, "Sheesh. These Beavertown drivers. They're the worst in the country. What number on Waterloo Row was that again, sir?"

"167."

"You must've booked a suite at 'Torren Executive Suites'."

"There must be a mistake. That address is a private residence."

"It was 'Willow Lane B & B' for many years until a couple of months ago. Now it's 'Torren Executive Suites' for politicians and other big shots in town for conferences, meetings and stuff."

"I didn't know that. I haven't been here for a while."

"You must've been away for a long time, sir."

"Yes. A long time."

"Welcome back."

"Thank you. There must be a lot of other changes I'm going to discover, as well."

"I hope you enjoy discovering them. Well, here we are. Is this the right house?" the cabbie parked in the driveway.

"Yes, it is...but...There used to be a smaller house – a bungalow – right there..."

"It burnt down a couple of months ago, sir."

"Was anyone hurt?"

"No sir. It had been vacant for a while...Do you want me to wait for you? I don't think you can get a suite here without booking ahead."

"Yes. Please wait for me." he walked up the front steps to the veranda and rang the doorbell. He waited for what felt like an eternity before a gray-haired woman opened the door.

"Yes? How can I help you?"

"Is this...still the Horncastle house?"

"The owner is a Horncastle. Do you have a reservation?"

"No...I didn't know it was converted...It used to be a private residence. I used to live here."

"Were you part of the staff?"

"No. I'm Jack Chandler."

"Sure you are. And I'm Meryl Streep."

"I am Jack Chandler. I can show you I.D."

"That doesn't prove anything. You could have the same name. I don't know what you're trying to pull here, but I suggest you move along."

"My cousin Dorothy Horncastle can verify my identity. Look, I have a cab waiting. Would you happen to have a suite available?"

"We do, in fact, have one on the second floor. Miss Horncastle doesn't like to rent that one out, unless there's overwhelming demand. I'm going to make an exception this time. I hope I don't live to regret it."

"Thank you. I promise you won't regret it. Let me get my luggage from the cab." he ran back to the taxi and removed his suitcases.

"Looks like you've got a room on short notice. You must have a way with the ladies." the driver said.

"Thanks for everything." Jack paid the driver and added a generous tip.

"Thank you, sir." the middle-aged man beamed, "Nice doing business with you."

The woman eyed Jack with suspicion as he checked in. She led him up the stairs, with a lanky young man in tow, struggling with Jack's luggage.

"This is it." she unlocked the door, "No smoking. No loud music. Dinner is served at six thirty, in the dining room, if you are interested. There's an additional charge."

"Thank you. If my day goes as planned, I may not be back by then."

"Suit yourself." she turned to leave as Jack tipped the bellhop.

Jack closed the door behind them. It was his old room! His very own room. His sanctuary. What a fortuitous turn of events in this bittersweet homecoming. Dottie's superior taste in decorating was evident in the elegant, traditional décor. The tacky mid-century pieces were gone. He hoisted his smaller bag on the bed and unlocked it. He removed a cotton bag with a green butterfly print and the word "*Kelebek*", the Turkish word for butterfly printed on it. He checked in it for the pastel and rainbow hued silk scarves and the evil eye jewellery wrapped in pink tissue paper. He folded the bag into a compact package and tucked it into the roomy inside pocket of his long wool coat. He locked the door behind him and descended the stairs. The woman was seated at the front desk in the atrium. She cast an icy glare in his direction. Once the door closed behind him, she picked up the receiver and dialed a number on her enormous and cumbersome Vista phone.

"Hey, Hazel, you'll never believe what just happened here...This man showed up right out of the blue. No reservation or anything. He said he thought this was still the Horncastle house. Then, he said he was Jack Chandler! Can you imagine that? He asked for a room, so I rented him that room Miss Horncastle doesn't like to rent out. I was so curious about this character, I wanted to keep an eye on him...Sure, I'll keep you posted about the developments...Gotta go now. Someone's coming down the stairs."

* * *

He walked briskly toward Queen Street. The crunching of the packed snow under his feet made it impossible to go unnoticed. Thankfully, the only people on Waterloo Row at this hour were retired seniors walking their dogs. He kept his head down, to avoid being recognized. Then, at the corner where Waterloo Row surrendered its identity to Queen Street, he was struck by an unfamiliar structure where his cherished club once had been: A Streamline Moderne masterpiece. The sign on it read: "Jack's Place". Tears filled his eyes. He quickened his steps. His heart throbbing, his hands trembling, he made his way to the familiar gray clapboard building. To his relief, the sign above the door was "Goldstein's Music Shop".

The door chime announced his arrival. An unfamiliar middle-aged woman turned around to greet him:

"May I help you, sir?"

"Yes. I'm looking for Sydney Goldstein." he stated.

"She's not in today. Would you like to leave a message?"

"Could you tell me where she lives?"

"I'm sorry, sir, but we can't give out that kind of information." the woman's face blanched in horror.

"Well, well, well, as I live and breathe!" Greeney emerged from the back room, "Jack Chandler in the flesh! I thought my ears were playing tricks on me!"

"THE Jack Chandler?" the other woman asked.

"The one and only."

"Hello, Greeney."

"I can see you have your memory back."

"At last. I came back immediately."

249

"Come here, you big lug." Greeney opened her arms, "Give me a hug."

He complied.

"You're looking good." Greeney stood back to study him, "A little on the skinny side, but we can fix that, can't we, Maxine?"

"We sure can. I'm Maxine, by the way. Nice to meet you, Mr. Chandler."

"Jack, please. Nice to meet you, too."

"This is Sydney's day off." Maxine informed him, "But she'll be back tomorrow."

"I don't think Jack wants to wait that long, Maxine." Greeney winked at her.

"How is she doing, Greeney?"

"She's doing well. She owns this place and "Jack's Place"."

"I saw it on the way here. What a magnificent building."

"She spared no expense, chose the architectural style for you. It changed hands and names a number of times along the way. Tony passed away quite a while back, I'm afraid."

"I knew that, though I couldn't remember him. A friend had a contact here. Greeney, is Sydney..."

"With someone?" Greeney completed his sentence, "No. She took Brett's passing very hard."

"Brett's passed away?"

"Yes. More than seven years ago."

"I'm so sorry. I had no idea."

"Sydney was just getting close to Warren, after his accident, but he died very suddenly back in August."

"Warren's gone, too?"

"Nothing's the way you left it, Jack."

"I guess I've been gone for too long. When I went to the house, I found out it's now a B & B for executives and a nasty woman is working at the front desk."

"That would be Maureen." Greeney laughed, "She's like a Doberman Pinscher."

"She didn't believe me when I told her who I was, but she did rent me my old room."

"That's kismet."

"Wait till Dottie finds out!" Maxine said.

"Where is she, anyway?"

"She's working at Peggy's old job and Peggy's a paralegal now, and she's taking courses to become a chartered accountant."

"Peggy's always been a smart cookie." Greeney said.

"I noticed the guest house is gone. Burnt down, the cab driver said. Where's Sydney living, then?"

"She hasn't lived there for eight years. She bought the house on Odell Avenue."

"The one Brett was renting?"

"Yes. The landlord was giving them trouble, so she bought it. They had a year together there. Just one year – but a glorious one. She nursed Brett right to the end through her cancer. When she lost her, she was inconsolable."

"They…"

"Yes. They were a couple."

"I'm glad they had each other. I'm sorry they had so little time together."

"After a seven year deep freeze, she was starting to thaw out with Warren, but, he, too, died too soon."

"Warren? That surprises me."

"The Warren you knew before you lost your memory evolved into a caring, just, compassionate man who fought hard to prove you were not dead, though your late mother staged an elaborate scheme to convince everyone you were, and even had a funeral for you. There's a tombstone with your name on it. There was a homeless man buried there. Warren hired investigators and exposed the murder of the homeless man orchestrated by your mother and late Uncle Willard. The date of death for you has since been removed from the headstone and the man has been buried elsewhere under his own name."

"Warren did all that?"

"Yes, and more. He exposed a woman claiming to be carrying Tony's child and most recently, a woman trying to swindle Sydney. He supervised the workers doing the renos at Sydney and Brett's house, so that Sydney and Brett could make one final visit to New York. About a year ago, he had a ski accident in

Colorado and lost the use of his legs. The guest house was renovated to accommodate his needs. After his death, it sat vacant until Halloween, when someone set fire to it."

"Did they ever catch the culprit?"

"Of course not. This is Beavertown, isn't it?"

"I'll put on some tea." Maxine said.

"Yes – come right through, Jack." Greeney motioned to him, "Let me prepare Sydney before you go over there. I don't want her to have a heart attack."

"I was hoping to surprise her, Greeney. She may not want to see me if she knows beforehand."

"Ye, of no faith. I'm sure she'll want to see you." she patted his shoulder.

"How did you get your memory back after all these years?" Maxine asked.

"I was in Istanbul, accompanying a friend who had been jilted by her girlfriend. She met up with a childhood friend to get caught up, and when the woman removed her scarf, I noticed her Star Of David necklace. Everything came flooding back."

"It had to take more than fifteen years and a trip across the world for you to get your memory back. Well, welcome back, Jack!"

"I'll get the minibites from the cupboard." Maxine offered.

"No, thank you. I'm too nervous to eat. I'll have to go to the florist and see what I can find on such short notice."

"Tell you what," Greeney said, "I'll call Benny down the street and ask him to put a rush order on an arrangement for you. I'm sure he'll oblige when he finds out it's you. "

"I appreciate that, Greeney."

"Tell me what kind of flowers you want, Jack, so I'll know what to tell him."

"Two dozen pink roses with baby's breath in a crystal vase. And, no card."

"You've got it. After that," she exchanged glances with Maxine, "I'd better call the boys, too, so they don't unwittingly disrupt the reunion."

"The boys?" Jack asked, "Do you mean Brett's boys?"

"No. Her kids are in Alberta." Maxine informed him in a low voice, leading him out of the office to allow Greeney to make her calls, "She means Eli and Dan."

"Who are Eli and Dan?"

"They are the nicest guys you could ever meet. Sydney was living in Toronto for a number of years and they were her neighbors and best friends. Actually, she met Eli first. Then, later, Dan was her therapist. Eli accompanied her to her appointments. He and Dan hit it off and became a couple. When Sydney's parents, aunt and uncle died, Jacob sold the house. So, the boys moved here to rent Maggie's old place, the guest house. They've been a tremendous source of support for her."

"I'm glad they came into her life. Thank you, Maxine."

"All set." Greeney was in the doorway of the office, "You can pick up the flowers in fifteen minutes and the boys are going to stay in their own place."

"I really appreciate everything, Greeney."

"Don't mention it. This is a momentous occasion. When you get settled in, we'll have a big celebration."

"I'd like that."

"Come on, have your tea and fill us in on what you've been doing for the past fifteen years."

*　*　*

He sat on a bench in the park with the best vantage point of her front door, where the floral arrangement awaited her. He glanced at his watch every thirty seconds. The bright, sunny winter's day was relinquishing its splendor to the mauve twilight. He wished she would return before darkness frightened away the last remnants of the sun. Then, all at once, there she was: Her wavy bob framing her soft features, her slim pocketbook hanging across her chest to free her hands, two plastic grocery bags on each side, weighing her down. She wearily climbed up the front steps to the porch. Upon her discovery of the flowers, she paused, placed her supermarket bags on the floor, and searched for a card without success. He leaped to his feet and began running across the street, calling out impetuously.

"Sydney! Sydney!"

She turned around as he reached the sidewalk and ran to her.

"Jack! It's you! It really is you!" a smile spread across her face.

"I came back the moment I remembered everything."

"You remember me." her tears were rolling down her reddened cheeks.

"I always remembered you, Sydney." his own tears were falling, "Even when I couldn't remember myself, I remembered you."

He caught her as she lost her footing and held her close, inhaling the scent of her hair. She sobbed in his arms.

"All these years, I've been dead inside." he kissed her hair and pressed her closer, "I can't exist without you in my life, Sydney. I'd understand if you don't want to be with me, but please let me be some part of your life – in any capacity."

"Jack...How could you ever think I wouldn't want to be with you?" she pulled away from his embrace to look at his face, her hands firmly on his arms.

"Sydney..." he pressed his cheek against hers, his tears blending with hers.

When she pulled away to wipe her tears with the tissue she retrieved from her coat pocket, he kissed her moist cheeks and licked her salty tears. Both of them laughed.

"Why don't we go inside?" she searched for her keys inside her pocketbook.

He took them from her and opened her door. She attempted to pick up the grocery bags, but he shook his head, picked them up and placed them in the front hall. He then brought the floral arrangement inside, locked the door and handed her the keys. She removed the wrapping paper from the flowers while he put away the groceries in the kitchen. They met up at the foot of the stairs and embraced. He clasped her hands and pressed them to his lips.

"I love you so much."

"I love you, too, Jack."

His lips sought hers. She moaned and kissed him fervently. Wriggling out of her coat, she tossed it on the floor. He fumbled with his buttons and retrieved the gift bag from his pocket before tossing his own coat and his jacket on the floor. He placed the gift bag on the hall table. She took his hand and led him up the stairs. He stood before her, trembling. She slipped off his tie and unbuttoned his shirt. He pulled her closer for a kiss, reaching under her sweater to unclasp her bra. She peeled off her V neck, palazzo pants and undergarments. He was still quivering before her. Her fingertips caressed his cheeks. He struggled with his shoes and pants. Then, he fell to his knees, wrapping his arms around her legs. His hands climbed up to the dark orchid he remembered so well. His mouth explored her salty caverns. His veins throbbed, as her screams filled the air. She gripped his hair as she came. He gazed up at her; she took his hands to lift him to his feet and led him to the foot of the bed. She knelt down and lowered his shorts. Her mouth closed on him. The flickering of her tongue sent him into spasms of ecstasy. He pulled out and threw her on the bed. He entered her with such force, she thought she might lose her mind from such pleasure.

Post coitus, he remained on top of her, his head resting between her breasts.

"I want to stay like this forever." he purred, "Never sleep, never eat, never go outside…I don't want to miss one single precious moment of being with you…I had to live without you for fifteen years. I can't bear the thought of a single millisecond away from you."

"Neither can I…I thought I'd never see you again, Jack."

"I wanted so desperately to be the man I used to be. I tried everything to remember, so I could come back to you. I couldn't let you see the pathetic shadow of a man I was reduced to."

"Jack, it wouldn't have mattered. I love you, no matter what."

"I loved you too much to let you end up stuck with me the way I was."

"I would never be 'stuck'. I would be grateful to have you back, no matter what."

"You were always with me…guiding me, cheering me on, supporting me. You were my guiding star, even though I thought I'd never regain my memory and be reunited with you. I carried you in my heart."

"Nothing and no one can tear us apart again. I promise you."

"And I promise I'll never do anything to hurt you again."

"Jack, what happened was not your fault. You didn't hurt me. Your mother hurt both of us."

"We lost so much time."

"Now, we can make up for all that lost time. We can build the life we envisioned. This time, free from your family's venom. Jack, you beat all the odds and regained your memory. That is a miracle. You and I are a miracle." she pulled the covers over them as he slid off her and nuzzled into her; yes, no one could touch them now.

EPILOGUE

"That was such a heart-rending story." Tilly dabbed at her eyes, "What happened after that? Did Jack and Sydney finally get to have a life together?"

"Yes. Jack had his Sydney for a little over twenty years until ovarian cancer took her away. After that, he sold the house to me with all its contents, and moved to a seniors' complex. He lasted about six months there and died of a broken heart."

"That's very sad. What happened to the others?"

"In chronological order: Maxine moved to Charlottetown to take care of her ailing mother. She's in constant touch. Olga got married and moved to Calgary. She sends Christmas cards every year. We lost Daniel to a heart attack. Greeney suffered a stroke following Leonard's death and spent some time at a seniors' care facility. We lost her last spring. Dottie took her own life this past Christmas Eve."

"Oh, I'm sorry!"

"She was bankrupt. The house went into foreclosure. She refused any help from me. I did all I could, to get her through the dark days, but she was despondent. She couldn't see a way out."

"I'm very sorry."

"Eli's at a seniors' facility and he's doing well, making friends, enjoying activities. I visit him regularly."

"I hope I can visit you from time to time, Peggy...Maybe even visit Eli with you. I feel I've missed so much...After my mother's death, her bogus parents dominated and smothered me and Dad; they cut me off from Sydney. I'll never forgive them for that...I loved her very much. So did Mom. But she never knew that...I'd like to visit her and Grandma's graves."

"Of course, love. I can show you where they're buried."

"I can't believe how ignorant people were to her about her name. Sydney's been a very popular girls' name since the late nineties. I'm so glad I didn't grow up during those earlier times. People were so judgmental and homophobic."

"I'm relieved our society has evolved – but not enough."

"What happened to the club and the music store?"

"Greeney's nephew Kirk owns the music store now. He bought the building, evicted the tenants on each side, the jewellery store and the insurance company, so he could expand in both directions. It's called 'Kirk's Music Box'. Cleo bought the club and divided it up. There's a restaurant on one side called 'Cleo's Fine Dining', and a banquet hall on the other side. What have you been doing all these years, Tilly?"

"I've been working in a medical office in John's Bay. About five years ago, I married a teacher like my dad. We're expecting a baby girl in four months. I plan to name her Sydney."

"I hope she'll grow up to be happier and luckier than her namesake, dear."

"Me, too."

"What brings you to Beavertown today, dear?"

"My dad wanted to visit one of his old teachers in the seniors' home on the North side. He heard he hadn't been well, so he wanted to see him, maybe for the last time. My husband and I came with him. They told me to phone them to tell them when and where to pick me up." she pulled her cell phone out of her purse.

"Why don't you call and tell them to come in and have tea with us?"

"Thank you. I will."

"While you're doing that, there's something I need to do."

When Peggy returned, she was carrying a large box.

"This is for you." she placed it on the floor in front of the sofa.

"For me?"

"They're old family photos. Sydney saved them for you. When she passed away, Jack gave them to me. I had no idea how to contact you. Your dad is not listed in the John's Bay phone book. I'm so glad you came to visit."

"Me, too. I hope you'll come to visit us in John's Bay, too."

"Of course I will."

"Now that I'm going to be a mother myself, I want to erase every trace of Emerald and Henry from our lives, and go back to being called Brette for a nickname instead of Tilly.”

“I’m glad. That’s what your mom wanted you to be called.”

“They’re all reunited on the other side…Mom, Grandma, Sydney, Jack, Dottie, Warren, Sydney’s parents, Daniel, Greeney, Maggie, Daisy…And I’m sure Tony visits them once in a while, too, even though he is with Adele.”

“Not to forget their friends from the club…Chuck, Johnny O., Gene And The Matchmakers…”

“Heaven must be one big party with that bunch around.”

“I’ll bet it is.”

“Some day, we’ll join them.”

“Until then, we’ll make the most of our lives here.”

ABOUT THE AUTHOR:

Summer Seline Coyle has a B.A. in Sociology and English Literature, and a Certificate in Counselling.

Her personal history of extreme abuse, neglect, and injustice is the driving force behind the empathy, tenderness, and passion in her portrayal of her diverse characters. Through her fiction, she hopes to raise public awareness, and be a healing voice for other survivors.

ALSO BY SUMMER SELINE COYLE:

DAISIES FROM ASHES

SCORPIONS HUNT BY NIGHT

SANDCASTLES IN THE RAIN

SUMMER IS A SHORT SEASON